Lights, Action, Lily!

Other Books Available

The Lily Series
  Here's Lily!
  Lily Robbins, M.D. (Medical Dabbler)
  Lily and the Creep
  Lily's Ultimate Party
  Ask Lily
  Lily the Rebel
  Lights, Action, Lily!
  Lily Rules!
  Rough & Rugged Lily
  Lily Speaks!
  Horse Crazy Lily
  Lily's Church Camp Adventure
  Lily's in London?!
  Lily's Passport to Paris

Nonfiction
  The Beauty Book
  The Body Book
  The Buddy Book
  The Best Bash Book
  The Blurry Rules Book
  The It's MY Life Book
  The Creativity Book
  The Uniquely Me Book
  The Values & Virtues Book
  The Year 'Round Holiday Book
  The Fun-Finder Book
  The Walk-the-Walk Book
  NIV Young Women of Faith Bible

the Lily series

Lights, Action, Lily!

Nancy Rue

ZONDERkidz

ZONDERVAN.com/
AUTHORTRACKER
follow your favorite authors

Lights, Action, Lily!
Copyright © 2002 by Women of Faith

Requests for information should be addressed to:
Zonderkidz, Grand Rapids, Michigan 49530

ISBN-13: 978-0-310-70249-8
ISBN-10: 0-310-70249-6

Published in association with the literary agency of Alive Communications, Inc., 7680 Goddard Street, Suite 200, Colorado Springs, CO 80920.
www.alivecommunications.com

Editor: Barbara Scott
Interior design: Amy Langeler
Cover design: Jody Langley
Cover illustrator: Laura Tallardy

Printed in the United States of America

07 08 09 10 11 12 • 18 17 16 15 14 13

Chapter 1

"I hate having my picture taken," Reni said. "I always look so stupid."

"You do not either look stupid," Lily said.

"Yes, I do." Reni crossed her eyes to prove it, then shrugged. "It doesn't matter how I look in my school picture, though. My parents are having my portrait done at a studio so I can be holding my violin."

Their friend Suzy looked at Reni in awe. Lily did too. Reni was, after all, her best friend, and everything she did was amazing as far as Lily was concerned.

"I guess it doesn't matter about my picture," Suzy said, tilting her head so that her very dark, straight hair splashed across her cheek. "My soccer pictures are always better than my school pictures."

"That's nice for you two," Lily said. "But this is the only set I'm getting. And they have to be good. My dad's putting all our pictures on this family tree thing he's making for my grandmother for Christmas. He's got pictures of people on there from a hundred years ago. They all look like this."

Lily stood up straight and stiff and stared sternly into an imaginary camera lens. Suzy giggled softly.

"Okay, what's so funny? Let me in on the joke."

The three girls jumped—and then grinned—well, at least Reni and Lily did. Suzy ducked her head behind Lily's shoulder. It was Officer Horn, better known in kid circles as "Deputy Dog." She kept order around Cedar Hills Middle School with her mud-brown, piercing stare and her thumbs hooked into her belt. Although the Girlz—Lily, Reni, Suzy, Zooey, and Kresha—had had their run-ins with her at the beginning of the year, she was their "bud" now—as long as they played by the rules. Deputy Dog didn't cut any slack to those who didn't.

"Do that face for her, Lily," Reni said.

Lily was about to when there was a shriek from the front of the line, up close to where the photographer was snapping pictures. Deputy Dog's ears practically stood on end.

"Excuse me, ladies," she said, and strolled toward the front.

Lily stood on her tiptoes to check out the action.

"What's going on?" Reni asked.

Lily groaned. It was, of course, Ashley Adamson and her clone-friend Chelsea. Shad Shifferdecker was up there holding what appeared to be Ashley's picture order form over his head, and Ashley was jumping for it and missing—on purpose, from what Lily could tell. *That girl is so boy crazy,* Lily thought, *it makes me want to reach for a barf bag.*

"Is it Ashley?" Reni said.

"Who else?"

"And Shad?"

"Uh-huh."

"Are they still going out?" Suzy said.

Lily rolled her eyes. "That's what she says. Where do people 'go' when they say they're 'going out'? I know Ashley's parents don't let her date. She's twelve!"

"I don't know," Reni said. "They let her get away with everything. Did you see how short her skirt is?"

"She'll get in trouble for that with Deputy Dog," Suzy said. And then she tugged anxiously at her own skirt.

"Even if they do let her date," Lily said, "who would want to go out with Shad Shifferdecker anyway? Blech!"

"He's getting cuter," Reni said.

"Gross! He's sure not getting nicer!"

"Shh, Lily!" Suzy whispered. "Deputy Dog's looking back here!"

Lily lowered her voice, and Reni and Suzy leaned their heads in. "Friday, when I forgot my lunch," Lily said, "and I had to go through the food line, he was standing behind me, pretending like he was pulling bugs out of my hair—and eating them!"

"That is *so* disgusting!" Reni said.

"It's definitely not cute," Lily said. She gave her mane of curly red hair a toss. "As soon as I got home, I got out the shampoo. It was like I could feel his cooties crawling around on my scalp."

Suzy shivered. Reni scratched her own head between two of her African black-beaded braids.

"Here she comes!" Suzy said, and ducked behind Lily again.

It was Ashley, sauntering from the picture-taking area and glancing over her shoulder while giving her turned-up blonde hair a flip.

"Move along, Adamson," Deputy Dog called to her in a bored voice. "The fans are not clamoring for more. You're finished here."

"Hel-lo-o! I'm waiting for Sha-ad," Ashley said.

"You're waiting to get yourself busted with that tone," Deputy Dog said. "Now get back to class."

Ashley rolled her eyes, threw her hair back, and stalked away.

As the line shuffled forward, Lily felt someone at her elbow and looked around to see Chelsea beside her.

"Did you forget it was picture day, Robbins?" Chelsea asked.

Lily could already feel her teeth clenching together. "No," she said.

"Oh—so you meant for your hair to look like that." She put her hands up, several inches from each side of her head, and said, "Poof!"

7

"You got a problem with that?" Reni said.

"No," Chelsea said. She curled her lip, leaving a trail of lip gloss under her nose. "But Robbins obviously has one. Ashley's right — she's so — *weird.*"

Then she swung herself around and at a fast walk went after Ashley, who was loitering in the gym doorway. Chelsea's short vinyl skirt twitched back and forth as she went.

"You're not weird, Lily," Suzy said. "I think you're beautiful."

"Thanks," Lily said.

She composed herself and turned to move ahead with the line. She knew better than to pay attention to Ashley, Chelsea, Bernadette, and the rest of the "popular" kids. And she knew she wasn't weird. Granted, she had the thickest, reddest, curliest hair in the whole school — and she was tall — and she got really into the things she was excited about. But that didn't make her *weird.* It just made her — *unique.*

Of course, right now she wasn't feeling particularly special, not after hearing about Reni's picture with her violin and Suzy's with a soccer ball.

Lily was at that point again — the point where she didn't have anything going that was just hers — that made her stand out — and it was even more obvious at home. Her older brother Art was already being asked to apply at different music schools, and he was only a junior. Her little brother Joe had enough sports trophies in his room to start his own store, and he was only ten. Even her parents were getting more and more recognition. Mom was taking over as head of the athletic department at the high school while the real guy was having surgery, and Dad had just submitted a book that was probably going to get published.

And here I am again, Lily thought. *I'm generic. I'm like the potato chips that come in the white bag with the black print — blah, bland, cardboard —*

"Lily — the line's moving," Reni said behind her.

Lily lurched forward into the space that had been left between her and Marcie McCleary. Marcie didn't seem to notice. She was too busy adjusting all the chains that were hanging from her jacket, from her arms, and out of the pockets of her too-big jeans.

Reni poked Lily and pointed to Marcie, her face a question mark. Lily knew what she meant, and she had the same question: *What is happening to Marcie? She's turning into a gang chick or something.*

Marcie's chain obsession also caught Deputy Dog's eye. "McCleary—come here—I want to talk to you," she said.

Marcie scurried over to her. Ahead, Shad was just taking his seat in front of the camera, and he was taking full advantage of Deputy Dog's turned-away head. Lily watched as he slouched on the stool, parked his arms on his thighs, and gave the photographer a "Whasup?" look. His snappy little eyes sparkled in the lights and for once didn't look so close together.

"Hey," Reni whispered, "he got his braces off. I told you he was getting cuter."

"Sit up, son," the photographer said.

Shad did—so straight he looked like he had a pole for a spine. Several kids ahead of Lily laughed appreciatively. Lily didn't.

"Not that straight," the photographer said. "Come on, give me something natural."

Shad grinned a half-grin, eyebrows arched up to the swish of hair that wasn't shaved. The photographer snapped the camera, and the kids in the front of the line clapped.

"That's gonna be *so* good!" some girl said.

"Oh, brother," Lily said.

There were only two people ahead of Lily now, and with Deputy Dog still preoccupied with Marcie and her chains, Shad shoved his hands into the pockets of his jeans, yanked them down below his boxers, and began to work the line. Lily folded her arms and turned her back in his direction.

That didn't keep Shad from stopping behind her. She could feel him investigating her curls.

"Touch it and you'll draw back a nub," Lily said.

"Ooh — I'm scared. I'm terrified," Shad said.

"Give it up, Shifferdecker," Reni said. "Move up, Lily — you're gonna be next."

Lily edged sideways so she didn't have to turn around and look at Shad. For all she knew, he had given up and left. She should be so lucky.

"I'm gonna wait and see how that hair looks under them lights," Shad said. "Wait — let me get my sunglasses out."

Lily ignored him and slid onto the stool. The photographer peered at her over the camera and said, "Smile, honey."

Lily did. Ever since last year when she'd gone to modeling school, she hadn't minded having her picture taken. But having Shad there definitely made it hard to concentrate.

"Help — help — I'm blind!" Shad said. "She blinded me!"

Crawl back into the hole you came out of, Lily thought. But she didn't just think it. She knew she looked it too, as she shot Shad a disdainful glare. The photographer chose that moment to snap the picture. Behind him, Reni and Suzy looked horrified.

"Next, please," the photographer said.

"But I wasn't ready!" Lily said. "I was looking over there and doing this!" She reenacted the face. By now, the kids behind Suzy and Reni were craning their necks like Gumby dolls and snickering.

"Can't you take it over?" Lily said.

"Nope," the photographer said. "Wait 'til these come out, and if you don't like them, you can come back for retakes."

"When's that gonna be?" Lily said.

"Middle of December."

"But —"

"Next, please?"

As Lily walked out of the light, she could feel the hot blotches on her face. That always happened when she got mad—and right now, she was surprised there wasn't steam coming out of her ears too. She stomped after Shad with her fists doubled, but he was nowhere in sight outside the gym. It figured. He'd seen Lily's temper in action before.

Lily, her mind reeling, stopped in the hallway and looked around. She had to get to class, but later—later, he was *so* gonna get it from her. She marched out of the gym wing and up the stairs toward Mrs. Reinhold's room, where a detention would be waiting if she didn't get there in what Mrs. R. called "a timely fashion."

Shad wasn't in that class—it was accelerated English, and Shad wasn't much of a student. Maybe that was a good thing, since strict Mrs. Reinhold (Mrs. Stranglehold, Ashley and her friends called her behind her back) wouldn't give Lily a chance to get back at him under her hawk eyes.

Lily was fuming about that as she rounded the corner and spotted Shad standing in the middle of the hall. He was obviously mimicking Lily's signature glare for his two friends—Daniel and Leo.

Lily clenched her fists and stomped up behind him. Leo and Daniel slunk off like a pair of weasels as Shad turned around to face Lily and began an evil grin that drew his beady little eyes close together over his nose.

"You are an absurd little creep," Lily said.

"Cool," Shad said.

"No, it is *not* cool. It is *so* not cool. That picture is going on a family heirloom, not that you care."

"Not that I even know what an air-loom is," Shad said. "It's goin' on the side of a plane? Cool—"

"No, moron! Forget it. But you are *so* paying for it if I have to have retakes."

"I ain't payin' for the camera—which you broke when you looked in it."

Lily narrowed her eyes at him and showed her teeth—kind of the way her dog Otto did when she made him drop a pen of hers he was chewing. Shad made the same face back—only uglier.

"You are so immature," she said. "My *dog* is more grown up than you are."

"Yeah?" Shad said. His eyes sparkled. "Well, *my* dog is better *lookin'* than you are. Come to think of it, my little sister's pet guinea pig is better lookin' than you are."

Lily maintained her narrow-eyed stare. "Anybody else?" she said.

"Nah—that's all the pets we got."

"I believe round one goes to the young man," said a voice from the doorway.

Lily froze. It was Mrs. Reinhold.

Chapter 2

That's it, Lily thought. *My life is over. I might as well just lie down right here in the hall and die.*

It didn't even help that Reni and Suzy appeared around the corner just then. There was no comfort when you were up against Mrs. Reinhold.

Lily turned to look at her, just as Mrs. Reinhold was motioning for Reni and Suzy to go on into the classroom. Then she stood over Lily and Shad and adjusted her teeny-weeny glasses. Shad looked at his feet, the smirk still on his face.

"Interesting little dialogue," Mrs. Reinhold said.

Lily opened her mouth to explain, but Mrs. Reinhold put up her hand.

"You," she said to Shad. "Where do you belong?"

Shad mumbled something out of the side of his mouth and continued to smirk at his shoes.

"Then go there," Mrs. Reinhold said.

Shad shrugged, shoved his hands into his pockets, and ambled off as if he were going window-shopping.

"I'm sorry if we were too loud," Lily said. "But he—"

Again, Mrs. Reinhold put her hand up. "I would like for you to meet me back here during lunch," she said. "Did you bring a sack lunch today?"

Lily could only nod.

"Good—bring that with you and we'll eat here."

"Okay," Lily said. She could feel her face wanting to crumple, and she willed herself not to cry until she was at least in her seat, behind a book or something.

"This is not a punishment, Lilianna," Mrs. Reinhold said. "There is just something I would like to speak with you about. Now—what was that young man's name that you were out here sparring with?"

That Lily was glad to tell her. If Shad had gotten off scot-free, she would have been beyond mad.

Mrs. Reinhold seemed to be locking the information into her memory as she nodded. "All right," she said. "Go on inside. The assignment is on the board."

Lily nodded and went for the door, but she stopped halfway there and looked back at Mrs. Reinhold. "I'm sorry. I really am. When we were—"

"Please, Lilianna," Mrs. Reinhold said. "You are such an obsessive child."

Lily didn't know what "obsessive" meant, but she was sure it couldn't be good. When she got to her desk, behind Ashley, she sank heavily into the seat.

"Busted," Ashley whispered over her shoulder.

Lily ignored her, although she would rather have Ashley hiss insults at her all day than be in trouble with Mrs. Reinhold. She had worked so hard to get her approval.

After class, Lily was answering Suzy and Reni's barrage of questions on the way to geography when they ran into Zooey and Kresha.

"Zooey—you look so cute!" Suzy said.

It was true. There was a time when Zooey had been the plump one in the group, but ever since the beginning of the school year, she'd been losing what she called her "baby fat." That meant having to get new clothes, and Zooey was decked out in them now. She looked like an ad for the Gap.

Zooey beamed and did a twirl so they could all take in the khaki outfit. All, that is, except for Kresha, who was frowning at her picture order form.

"What's wrong?" Lily said.

"I can no understand dis," Kresha said. "What this means — *g-e-n-d-e-r?*" She scowled at Lily from beneath her sandy-brown bangs.

"That means whether you're a boy or a girl," Lily said.

Kresha looked at the form and frowned again. "This say *M* or *F*."

"Male or female."

"Oh," Kresha said. Her smile lit up her face and then faded again. "What I am?" she said.

Zooey slapped her hand over her mouth to keep from giggling, but Suzy poked her in the side anyway. They were all careful not to hurt Kresha's feelings. She was Croatian, and although she was doing well with her English, it was still a struggle for her sometimes.

"You're female," Lily told her. "Boys are male. Boys are also idiots, and I can't stand them."

"Oh," Kresha said. She squinted at the form. "That is on here?"

"No — Lily's just venting," Reni said.

"What happened?" Zooey said, her big eyes wide.

"She can tell you at lunch," Suzy said, glancing nervously at her watch.

"I won't be at lunch," Lily said. "Mrs. Reinhold wants to see me."

The four faces in front of her looked stricken.

"Yeah," Lily said. "I know."

Fourth-period geography class usually dragged because their young teacher Ms. Ferringer was so unorganized, but that day it went by all too quickly. When the bell rang, Lily felt her stomach tying itself into knots.

Reni passed her a Girlz-Gram before she rushed off to the orchestra room for practice, and Lily read it as she dragged herself to Mrs. Reinhold's room.

You were right. Shad was wrong. Tell Mrs. R. It'll be okay.

—Reni

Although it was written in the Girlz usual telegram style, it did make Lily feel a little better as she pulled open the door to Mrs. R.'s room. Lily was always good at explaining things. Maybe it *would* be okay.

She was a little stunned, however, when she walked into the room and saw six other people there.

Wow, Lily thought. *Mrs. Reinhold must have radar or something to get this many people for lunch detention.*

It was odd, though, because she recognized most of the kids as being eighth graders, and Mrs. Reinhold taught mostly seventh grade except for the accelerated eighth-grade English class. These weren't the kind of kids that usually got into trouble.

Lily grunted to herself. *I'm not either!* she thought. *From now on, I'm never going to speak to Shad Shifferdecker again. I'm going to pretend he doesn't exist.*

She was counting up the number of times she had made that vow to herself when Mrs. Reinhold said, "All right people, listen up. Is everyone here?"

It wasn't actually a question you answered, although one rather chubby eighth-grade boy did raise his hand and say, "I am!"

16

"Thank you, Philip," Mrs. Reinhold said dryly. She counted kids with her finger and frowned. "I'm missing one."

"No, you're not," Philip said, pointing to the door.

Shad was just sauntering in. Lily turned her head sharply so she wouldn't have to look at him.

"Good. I'll get started," Mrs. Reinhold said. "Listen carefully to what I'm about to tell you because I only have time to explain it once. As you will see, time is of the essence. If when I am finished you decide that you do not want to participate in the program, you may opt to leave at that time."

Lily hoped she didn't look as confused as she felt. This was a weird kind of detention—

"Now, then," Mrs. Reinhold said. "I have chosen promising students from my classes—as well as one I selected off the street."

She gave Shad a pointed look, and to Lily's disgust he raised a fist as if he'd just won an Olympic gold medal.

"I am asking you," Mrs. Reinhold went on, "to participate in a pilot program that is being done district-wide to encourage students to study Shakespeare."

"What's that?" Shad asked.

She gave him a Reinhold glare. He slumped down in the seat. Lily rolled her eyes.

"Shakespeare, as most of you know, was a great Renaissance playwright who left us some of the richest, most enduring plays in the English language."

Shad pretended to snore. If Mrs. Reinhold heard him, she didn't let on.

"Each participating school is to choose a group of students who will put together scenes from a Shakespearean play and perform them at a festival on November 20."

"Do we get out of school to go to this thing?" said a boy with a ponytail that cascaded down from a partially shaved head.

"No—it's a Saturday, Wesley," Mrs. Reinhold said.

Shad bolted up in his seat. "A Saturday?" he said.

"You will note that the date is only three weeks away," Mrs. Reinhold went on. "I received the word late, and that is why I have hand-picked students myself rather than holding auditions."

"I gotta do school stuff on a Saturday?" Shad said.

"I know most of you well enough to see that you are bright, capable, creative—"

"I ain't workin' on no Saturday—"

"—and have some natural acting ability."

Mrs. Reinhold looked at Shad, who stopped in the middle of another protest against working weekends and let half a grin appear.

"Acting ability?" he said.

"Yes," Mrs. Reinhold said.

She left Shad puzzling over that and continued. "I have already cast the roles, and I have your scripts ready. If you are going to participate in this program, you will be expected to be here during lunch every day between now and the twentieth. You will be expected to learn lines and take direction from college theater students who are coming in to assist us."

"This sounds hard," said a girl with glasses and a slightly off-center ponytail.

"It is definitely challenging," Mrs. Reinhold said.

"I'm outta here then," Shad said.

"The college students are coming in to teach you how to do stage combat choreography. To use the vernacular, you will learn how to throw each other around on stage."

Shad stopped halfway out of his desk and grinned again. "You mean, like fights and stuff?" he said.

"Yes," Mrs. Reinhold said.

Shad said, "All right!"

Next to him a kid with a completely shaved head held up his hand for Shad to give him a high five.

"Gary, Shad," Mrs. Reinhold said, "if you have finished the formalities."

Gary grinned. Shad looked baffled.

Oh, brother, Lily thought with an inner groan. *Shad doesn't even know what formalities are. He oughta be just great at Shakespeare.*

She'd never actually read any of Shakespeare's plays herself, but she'd heard Dad talk about them—he was an English professor, after all—and she knew they had a lot of hard words and fancy language. It *would* be a challenge—for Lily. For Shad, she was sure it would be impossible.

"Our scenes will be taken from *The Taming of the Shrew*," Mrs. Reinhold said, "which is one of Shakespeare's comedies. We will be doing three scenes."

She picked up several sets of papers from her desk, and everyone in the room sat up straighter in their seats—except for Shad, who played a soft rendition of "Wipe Out" on the desktop with his fingers. But he was watching Mrs. Reinhold intently.

"Before I hand these out," she said, "let me ask if there is anyone who would rather not participate in this program. There will be no penalty for excusing yourself—I know Shakespeare is not for everyone—but my firsthand knowledge of each of you indicates to me that you are all up to this challenge."

Lily stared at her. How did Mrs. Reinhold know anything about Shad? Until a few hours ago, she didn't even know his name.

"Now then," Mrs. Reinhold said, "this first scene is for four males—but because we have a plethora of girls, I am asking two of you young ladies to play the parts of old men. You will be costumed complete with mustaches, beards, whatever it takes to transform you."

I don't really want to play an old man, Lily thought. She was already envisioning herself at center stage in a gorgeous Renaissance gown dripping with gold braid. She held her breath.

"Fiona," Mrs. R. said to an African-American girl who was even skinnier than Kresha, "would you and Natalie take these crossover parts?"

Fiona didn't look any too pleased, and neither did Natalie, the girl with the glasses and the crooked ponytail. At least—they didn't until Mrs. Reinhold handed the next script to Gary, the kid with the shaved head. Reni would have said he was "cute." They also seemed to like Philip, the chubby kid, and the four of them shoved their desks together and began to whisper excitedly. Lily looked around. She didn't know Wesley or the other girl, a pretty, dimpled eighth-grader whose blonde hair was cut in a perfect bob. She wondered if either one of them would be very excited about working with her.

"Wesley, you and Hilary will work together as Bianca and Lucentio."

"Who are they?" Hilary said, taking the script as if it were a poisonous snake.

Lily didn't hear the answer. She was frozen to the seat. The only two people left were herself—and Shad.

"Ah—you two," Mrs. Reinhold said. It was rare to see her smile, but she was beaming broadly at Shad and Lily, as if she were enjoying some joke nobody else understood. Lily certainly didn't get it.

"Shad," she said, "you will play the part of Petruchio. Lilianna— you will be Katharina—better known as Kate."

"Are we in the same scene?" Lily said.

Mrs. Reinhold's eyebrows twisted. "Yes—unless you each want to do a monologue."

"What's a monologue?" Shad said.

"When you have a long piece to say by yourself," Mrs. Reinhold said.

"Forget that—no way." Shad took the script and then suddenly looked up. "Hey," he said. "I gotta do this with Snobbins?"

He jerked his head toward Lily.

"With Lilianna?" Mrs. Reinhold said. "Yes. And from what I saw out in the hall this morning, I think you two are perfectly matched for this scene."

Lily stared from her to the script and back again, until Mrs. Reinhold wandered over to one of the other groups. Lily looked at the writing in italics at the top of the scene.

Petruchio has come to convince Katharina to marry him.

Lily sagged all the way down in her seat.

Mrs. Reinhold had been wrong. This *was* a punishment.

Chapter 3

The Girlz met as usual after school that day in Zooey's basement, which had been transformed into a clubhouse for their meetings when the playhouse in Reni's backyard had gotten too small for them. Lily usually loved hanging out with the Girlz there, but that day as she flopped into the hot-pink beanbag chair, all she could think about was her Shakespeare-Shad dilemma. She tossed the script on the floor beside her, and Kresha picked it up and cocked her head at it.

She can probably understand it better than Shad will, Lily thought miserably, *and she barely speaks* modern *English!*

"I had this great idea today after I got my picture taken," Zooey said as she set a bowl of microwaved popcorn on the floor. "We oughta all put our pictures on the front of a scrap-book and then fill up the inside pages with other pictures and stuff about all the things we do together."

"Kind of like a Girlz Only Club yearbook," Suzy said.

Reni looked at Lily. "You think you're gonna want your school picture on the cover, though?"

"Reni!" Zooey said.

"You didn't see the look on her face when the photographer snapped it," Reni said.

"Nobody looks their best when they're staring at Shad Shifferdecker," Suzy said.

"It's up to you, Lil," Reni said.

Lily just shrugged.

"Don't you even like the scrapbook idea?" Zooey said.

"Yeah, it's fine," Lily said. "But I have worse things to worry about."

"Are you talking about that thing with Shad—that Shakespeare thing?" Reni said.

Kresha held up the script. "This?"

"Yeah," Lily said. "I really want to do this project—it sounds so cool, and I always wanted to be on a stage—"

"Not me," Suzy said. She puckered her eyebrows as if she were at that moment standing in the wings, waiting to go on. "I would be so scared I wouldn't be able to open my mouth."

"That's not a problem for Lil," Reni said.

She gave Lily a playful punch, but Lily just sighed.

"Come on," Reni said. "It's not worth it if you have to work with Shad. He's always been hateful to you."

"It would be worth it if I could do the scene with somebody else."

Zooey and Suzy nodded sadly. Kresha was busy frowning over the script again.

Reni stretched out on the neon-green beanbag chair she always sat in and munched thoughtfully on a mouthful of popcorn.

"What?" Lily said.

"I don't see how it's that big of a deal," Reni said.

"What? Working with Shad? Reni, he's evil!"

"No—doing the project at all. I mean, it's not like me wanting to do some solo or something. I'm gonna be a professional violinist. But you're not gonna be, like, this famous actress, so it's not gonna matter a week from now."

"Reni!" Zooey said.

Suzy put her hand on Lily's arm, and even Kresha looked up. Lily felt as if a bee had stung her—a bee on the end of Reni's tongue.

"It *is* a big deal," Lily said.

Reni poked a finger in and out of one of her dimples, a sure sign that she was trying to think of what to say to get her foot out of her mouth. "Okay," she said finally, "if it means that much to you, why don't you just talk to Mrs. Reinhold?"

"And why don't I just put my finger in that electric socket over there?" Lily said. She could feel her face going blotchy.

"Mrs. Reinhold likes you, though," Suzy said.

"She must," Zooey said, "or she wouldn't have asked you to be in this program thing."

Lily gave her a look. "She asked Shad too."

"Oh," Zooey said.

"Just tell her how Shad messes around all the time," Reni said, "and how he's always getting in trouble with Deputy Dog and stuff. You know Mrs. Reinhold—she's not gonna want somebody like that around."

"You really think?" Lily said.

"I *know*," Reni said.

Even Suzy nodded.

"Do it, Lily," Zooey said. "Hey—anybody wanna see the other new clothes I got this weekend?"

Through the rest of the meeting, Lily tried to concentrate on Zooey's wardrobe, but all she could really think about then, and later at the dinner table at home, was what she was going to say to Mrs. Reinhold. That is, until Dad announced his good news.

They were having dessert—a rare thing in their house. Mom usually had to fix dinner every night while running a load of laundry, opening the mail, and refereeing the squabbles that broke out among

Lily, Joe, and Art. But that night, everybody got a wedge of apple pie (Mrs. Smith's — but nobody cared) with ice cream. Joe and Art dug in like they might never see dessert again, but Lily looked suspiciously at her mother.

"What's going on?" she said.

Instead of answering, Mom tapped her spoon on the side of her water glass and said, "Attention, everyone. Your father has an announcement to make."

"You're finally gonna get a pair of glasses that'll bring you into the twenty-first century!" Art said. "All right, Dad!"

"You're gonna get rid of the van and buy a Porsche!" Joe said.

Mom raised a brown sugar-colored eyebrow. "Did I say we were going to play Twenty Questions?" she said. "Your *father* would like to speak."

"Go ahead, Daddy," Lily said.

She felt Joe kick her under the table, but she didn't look at him. She knew he'd be mocking her. She and Art could pretty much communicate now without spitting at each other, but Joe was still another story. He was *so* ten.

Dad's blue-like-Lily's eyes sparkled behind his glasses, and Lily knew this had to be something good. Most of the time, Dad had kind of a vague look because most of the time, he was thinking about C. S. Lewis or Shakespeare or some book Lily didn't even know existed yet. Right now, even his fading-red hair seemed to be standing up with excitement.

"What gives, Dad?" Art said. "Dish."

"I'm happy to tell you," Dad said, "that my book has been accepted for publication. It will be out in six months."

"All right!" Art said.

Lily got up and hugged his neck.

Joe grinned and said, "Did Dad write a book?"

"Tell them the rest," Mom said.

Suddenly, Dad looked shy. "The money that I will receive up front—it's called an advance on royalties. You see, the way this works—"

"Dad," Art said, "you can give us a lesson in publishing later. How much are we talking?"

Mom and Dad exchanged one of those glances that meant they were having a conversation without words.

"Quite a bit," Dad said.

"Are we gonna be rich?" Joe said.

"Like it matters!" Lily said to him. Then she turned to Dad. "Are we?"

"Obviously we're going to be somewhat richer than we are right now," Dad said.

"But that isn't all," Mom said.

"There's more?" Art said.

"More money?" Joe said.

"I've been promoted to full professor," Dad said. "I now have tenure."

"What's that?" Joe said.

"That means they can't fire him unless he mugs a student or something," Art said.

Mom's mouth twitched. "Something like that," she said.

"Does it mean you get a raise?" Joe said.

"Yes, it does."

"Dude!" Joe said. "So—now you actually could buy a Porsche." Joe's brown eyes were gleaming. "And you could give it to me when I'm sixteen."

"In your dreams, Squatty Body," Art said. "I happen to be the oldest son and therefore the heir to—everything that's worth anything."

"No, you are not!" Lily said. "We get to split everything evenly—don't we, Mom?"

"I can't believe I'm hearing this from you kids," Dad said. "You sound like a bunch of moneymongers."

"What's a monger?" Joe said.

"A greedy little punk like you," Art said.

"And you!" Lily said.

"And, let's not leave out little old—*you*," Art said.

"STOP."

They did. Dad didn't get stern too often, but when he did, the Robbins kids put on their brakes. His eyes were sharp as he looked at each one of them. Lily could feel her throat getting tight.

"Sorry, Dad," she said.

"Me too," he said. "Very sorry to see that my children have become so materialistic." He took off his glasses and chewed on the earpiece as he looked at each one of them again. It was times like this when Lily wished he would just put everybody on restriction and let it go. Sitting there while he looked disappointed was the worst.

"It *is* fun to have nice things," Dad said. "Otherwise, we would dress you three in rags and send you off to school looking like the homeless."

Lily wanted to comment that Joe looked like that most of the time anyway, but she bit her lip.

"However," Dad went on, his voice still heavy, "I think it would be much more fitting for us to share our good fortune with someone who isn't as blessed as we are for whatever reason."

"Oh," Joe said. "So I guess a Porsche is out of the question, huh?"

"Completely," Dad said. "We're going to put the money to good use somehow. We're praying about what that should be, and we hope you kids will pray too."

"Of course," Lily said.

"Sure, Dad," Art said.

"I got an idea already," Joe said. "You could give your Honda Accord to somebody that doesn't even have a car—and *then* you could buy a Porsche."

"Where did this one come from?" Dad said to Mom.

"Beats me," Mom said. "I thought *you* knew."

Later as Lily was propped up in bed with her dog Otto and her journal, she wrote about what God might want Mom and Dad to do with all that money.

I wish they could just buy me my own theater so I could have anybody in a play that I wanted — and not *have anybody I* didn't *want.*

That made her sound as selfish as Joe, so she added, *But since that's wrong of me, God, could you just help me tomorrow when I talk to Mrs. Reinhold about Shad? I want to be in the scene a lot — especially since she gave me a special one — but it's gonna be impossible with Shad. Will you help me know what to say?*

She closed the journal and chewed on her pen while Otto eyed it hungrily. She suddenly felt uneasy, the way she did when she wasn't sure she'd done all her homework, or that she'd answered number five right on the test she'd just turned in.

"Something's wrong, Otto," she said as she rolled over to turn off the light. "I don't think God's all that happy with what I just wrote."

She sighed as she snuggled in under the covers, with Otto burrowing down to get in the crook of her knees. She wasn't sure *why* God wouldn't be happy, but she had learned one thing from all her past mistakes: If it didn't feel right, she'd better pay attention.

Lily got a ride with Mom the next morning so she could catch Mrs. Reinhold before school. She'd tried practicing her speech for Otto while she was getting dressed, but he hadn't been much help. All he wanted to do was pull stuff out of her backpack—and he did manage to chew the zipper so she couldn't close it up all the way.

Just what I needed this morning when I want to be all calm and mature in front of Mrs. Reinhold, she thought as she hurried through the main part of the building toward the stairs. She was about to take the first step up when she heard angry voices above her. She hesitated.

"You are *so* not doing that thing with *her!*" she heard a girl say.

Yikes, Lily thought. *That's Ashley!*

She listened harder, but all she heard in return was a grunt.

"I mean it," Ashley went on. "If you have to act like she's your girlfriend on the stage—well, you're just not gonna, that's all there is to it!"

Another grunt.

"I mean it, Shad!"

Shad? Lily suddenly felt sick. The "her" Ashley was talking about was Lily.

"You're not gonna get all lovey-dovey and talk me out of it either," Ashley said. "Don't touch me!"

"That's right, Shifferdecker—don't touch her," said another voice that was clearly Deputy Dog's. "No physical contact of any kind is allowed on this campus."

"I wasn't touchin' her," Shad said.

"Good. See that you don't. And you two save your lovers' quarrels for someplace else. There's no yelling in these halls."

"I wasn't yellin'," Shad said.

There was a slight pause, during which Lily could imagine Deputy Dog putting her hands on her hips and getting closer to Shad's face, eyes narrowed into points.

"You're already walking on thin ice with me, Shifferdecker," Deputy Dog said. "I can haul you in right now if you want."

"Nah," Shad said.

"Then keep your voices down and your hands off each other, or it's automatic suspension for both of you. You're too young for the relationship thing anyway. What are you, twelve?"

"I'm gonna be thirteen in January," Shad said. "I'll remind you so you can get my present."

"Don't hold your breath," Deputy Dog said.

Lily was definitely holding hers. She'd expected a major explosion from Officer Horn over Shad's attitude. He was obviously more afraid of Ashley than he was of her.

If Shad's really afraid of Ashley, she thought, *he probably won't even do the scene. I might not have to talk to Mrs. Reinhold about him after all.*

It was an attractive enough thought to make her change directions and head for the bench where the Girlz always met in the mornings.

30

Yeah — by lunchtime, Shad-doing-Shakespeare should be a thing of the past.

When Lily got to the meeting place, Zooey and Kresha were already there. Kresha was sitting on the bench watching Zooey as she strode back and forth wearing yet another new outfit. This one included a sizzling yellow top that made Zooey's face glow.

"Lily!" Zooey said when she saw her. "Do you know what?"

"No," Lily said as she joined Kresha on the bench.

Zooey sent the ponytail on the top of her head swinging back and forth. "Bernadette just went by — you know, that new girl that's really popular already?"

"Yeah," Lily said. She'd had dealings with Bernadette, and they hadn't been pretty.

"She was going by, like to her locker or something, and she stopped and looked at me — didn't she, Kresh?"

Kresha confirmed it with a nod.

"And she goes, 'Nice outfit. That's really cute. Where did you get it?' "

"Wow," Lily said. She tried to sound enthusiastic. After all, Zooey looked as if she were about to pop. Who wanted to be the one to stick a pin in that?

"And *then*," Zooey said, executing a twirl, "Chelsea goes by — and she looks at me once, and then she looks at me again like she just figured out who I was, and she goes, '*You* have lost *so* much weight. You actually look *good* in that outfit. Is it from the Gap?' " Zooey had to pause for a gurgle. "And I go, 'No, it's DKNY.' And she was all, 'Oh, isn't that what college kids wear?' And she wasn't even being mean, Lily. I think she's getting nicer."

Beside Lily, Kresha grunted.

"What?" Lily said to her.

"I do not think she is nicer," Kresha said.

Before Lily could even ask her what that meant, Zooey gave a squeal.

"Here comes Ashley!" she said. "Let's see what *she* says."

Zooey struck a casual pose, but as Ashley stormed up to them, she didn't appear to notice the outfit. She didn't even seem to notice Zooey, for that matter. Everybody there could have been invisible—except Lily—whom Ashley bore down on like a ticked-off goose. She was practically hissing.

"You!" she said when she came to a standstill over Lily. "Robbins! Stand up!"

"No," Lily said.

She started to turn away, but Ashley grabbed her roughly by the arm and yanked her to her feet. Lily could feel Kresha standing up behind her.

Lily pulled her arm away and glared coolly at Ashley—but her heart was already pounding and she could feel her face going blotchy.

"What?"

"You know 'what'!" Ashley said. "Duh—hel-lo—the love scene you're doing with Shad!"

Kresha peeked her head around Lily's side. "It is no a love scene—"

"Who asked you, you little alien?" Ashley said.

Lily heard Zooey whimper and Kresha start to breathe like a baby locomotive.

"It's okay, you guys," Lily said.

"It is *so* not okay!" Ashley said. "Shad is *my* boyfriend—he's going out with *me*—so you better keep your stinking hands off of him. Have you got that?"

Lily's mind raced to the finish line. "So tell him you don't want him doing the scene," she said. "He'll do anything you say."

For an instant, Ashley looked blank. It would have been the instant to hightail it out of there, but Lily wasn't quick enough. It passed, and Ashley curled her lip so far it nearly went up her nostrils.

"You'll do anything I say too, if you know what's good for you, Robbins," she said. *"No* little weirdo like *you* is going to lay one hand — one finger — on my boyfriend, or it's gonna get ugly."

With that she tossed her flippy hair and turned. Poor Suzy chose that moment to appear, and Ashley knocked hard against her shoulder as she passed her. Suzy looked as terrified as if she'd been grazed by an eighteen-wheeler.

"Oh no!" Zooey said, voice wavering. "What are you gonna do, Lily?"

"You do not pay no attention to her, Lily," Kresha said.

"It's kinda hard not to," Zooey said. "Especially when she tries to mow you down."

"Are you okay, Suzy?" Lily said.

Although she looked as if she could have used some CPR, Suzy nodded.

"Wow," Zooey said, eyes wide. "No wonder Shad's afraid of her — no wonder he'll do anything she says."

But Lily shook her head. "I don't think so. I heard her tell him he couldn't do the scene, but it looks like he's going to anyway, or she wouldn't have come down here threatening me."

"Oh yeah, huh?" Zooey said.

Suzy knitted her eyebrows at Lily. "Does this mean you're not going to be in the play?" she said.

"No," Lily said. "It means I have to go talk to Mrs. Reinhold."

There was nobody but Mrs. Reinhold in the room when Lily got there. She was straightening the desks into perfect rows, which reminded Lily to be careful about her grammar as she presented her case.

"Good morning, Lilianna," Mrs. Reinhold said as she swept to the front of the room, glasses swaying on their chain around her neck. "I can see you have something on your mind. Have a seat."

33

"I'm not trying to be a tattletale or anything," Lily said as she sank into the chair next to Mrs. Reinhold's desk, "but I can see how important this Shakespeare project is to you, so I thought I ought to tell you about Shad Shifferdecker. He could turn out to be a real problem."

Lily wasn't sure, but she thought she saw a smile flicker in Mrs. Reinhold's eyes.

"Now what on earth would make you think that?" Mrs. Reinhold said.

"Well, see, I've been going to school with him since kindergarten, and he has always been—"

"Lilianna," Mrs. Reinhold said. "I was being humorous."

"Oh," Lily said.

"I know that young Mr. Shifferdecker has his issues, and I am certain I can deal with those."

"If anybody can, it's you," Lily said quickly, "but he's not like any of the kids in our class. He's way worse."

" 'Way worse'?" Mrs. Reinhold said.

"A lot worse. Much worse. He's really bad."

"Understood," Mrs. Reinhold said. She sat up straighter in the chair the way people did when a conversation was almost over. Lily's heart sank. "I appreciate your concern, Lilianna," she said, "but I assure you that I have already taken Shad's propensity to misbehave into consideration. Today at our rehearsal, he will be asked to sign a contract—in fact, you all will—which states that he is to meet certain behavioral expectations, both in rehearsal and elsewhere in the school."

"But what if he messes up?" Lily said. "What happens then?"

"He is dropped from the program."

"But that means I would have to drop out too, since we're doing the scene together."

Mrs. Reinhold stood up then—which meant the conversation was *really* over. "Instead of working yourself into a frenzy about possible problems," she said, "I suggest you concentrate on making this the most positive experience possible, for you *and* for Shad."

Lily knew if she argued with Mrs. Reinhold, she was likely to be booted out of the program—and that just couldn't happen. The vision of bowing to thunderous applause was already so clear in her head she could *smell* it.

She hiked her backpack over her shoulder and went slowly for the door.

"Lilianna," Mrs. Reinhold said.

Lily stopped and turned around.

"You are a talented student in many ways," she said, "but it is time you learned something about process and teamwork. Let those be your goals in this project."

"I will," Lily said.

She had no idea what *process* meant, but all the way to her locker, she prayed she would figure it out—and soon.

Chapter 5

Even as she was on her way to Mrs. Reinhold's room for lunchtime rehearsal, Lily was still hoping that Ashley had convinced Shad to quit, but Shad was already there when she arrived. He was playing around with a purple velvet hat that looked like a throw pillow without the stuffing, decorated with a large fluffy feather. He plopped the thing on his head and pranced around the room, and then took a leap and stood on one of the desks, one foot on the desktop.

Mrs. Reinhold's dry voice came out of the corner where she was talking to some people Lily didn't recognize. "Mr. Shifferdecker," she said. "There will be plenty of opportunities for you to climb on furniture when you do your scene. For the time being, please use it as it was intended."

Shad jumped down and picked up the desk. "For firewood?" he said.

"No," she said. "For your behind. Sit."

To Lily's amazement, he did, still wearing the hat. And to her further amazement, Mrs. Reinhold just turned back to the people she was talking to, as if Shad had not just broken a big-time Reinhold Rule.

Lily sank heavily into her own desk. All hope was gone. Shad was obviously there to stay.

Mrs. Reinhold got up and shushed everyone and handed each kid two pieces of paper stapled together.

"What's this?" Shad said as he took his.

"This is a manhole cover, Mr. Shifferdecker," Mrs. Reinhold said. "We will be playing tiddlywinks with it shortly."

Shad grinned. "Cool," he said. Then he and Gary, the kid with the shaved head, high-fived each other.

Lily took the paper, which said, SHAKESPEARE PROJECT CONTRACT at the top. As her eyes ran down the page, she could feel herself sagging more with every sentence. It was just as Mrs. Reinhold had told her—an agreement that they would be at all the rehearsals, learn their lines, and behave themselves. It even said they'd be dropped from the program if they got into any trouble anywhere else in the school and had to be suspended.

There's no way Shad's gonna make it three weeks without getting in trouble, Lily thought. *He might as well quit right now.*

"You will notice," Mrs. Reinhold was saying, "that the word 'Shakespeare' is printed at the top of your contract. Study it carefully. If you are going to participate in this drama, you should be able to spell its author." She looked at them all over the top of her teeny-weeny glasses. "There will be a quiz."

"What if we flunk it?" Shad said.

"If you cannot spell the name, you cannot wear the hat."

Shad clutched at his headpiece and scowled at the contract, lips moving over the letters of Shakespeare's name.

You are so gonna lose that hat, Lily thought. *You can barely spell your own name.*

Next Mrs. Reinhold told them the story of *The Taming of the Shrew* so their scenes would make sense to them. She said that a *shrew* was like a spoiled brat, only grown up, and the character Katharina was the shrew in the play. Everybody, of course, looked at Lily.

"I'm not that way in real life," Lily said.

"Yes, Lilianna," Mrs. Reinhold said. "That's why it's called acting."

Lily saw Natalie and Fiona give each other the seventh-graders-are-such-geeks nudge.

"Katharina has a younger sister," Mrs. Reinhold went on. "A beautiful young lady with a sunny disposition. That would be Bianca."

She nodded at Hilary, who smiled smugly.

"There are plenty of men, both young and old"—Mrs. Reinhold glanced at Natalie and Fiona and Gary—"who want to marry Bianca, but no one wants to marry Katharina for obvious reasons." Mrs. Reinhold paused. "I have always felt that Katharina is the way she is because no one understands her. We grow to like her more as the play goes on."

That made Lily feel a little better.

"Katharina and Bianca's father, played by Philip—"

Philip got halfway up and gave an exaggerated bow.

"—sees the perfect opportunity to get both of his daughters married off. He says no one can marry Bianca until Katharina is married, and in the meantime, he's going to keep Bianca at home concentrating on her studies and her music until a suitable husband is found for Katharina. All of Bianca's suitors—"

"What's a suitor?" Shad said.

"A boyfriend."

"Why don't they just say that?" Shad said.

Lily stifled a groan. This was going to be worse than she thought.

"All of Bianca's suitors," Mrs. Reinhold went on, "are in despair because they don't see how that's ever going to happen. But along comes a man with a vision—and his name is Petruchio."

"Hey," Shad said. "That's me!"

He stood *all* the way up to take his bow, complete with much swishing of the purple hat. Lily noticed the two people Mrs. Reinhold had been talking to whispering to each other and nodding toward Shad. It was embarrassing to have visitors in there seeing him make a fool of himself.

"Petruchio sees something in Katharina that no one else does, and he also recognizes that along with Katharina comes a large dowry." Mrs. Reinhold looked at Shad. "A dowry is the money or property a father gives his daughter's new husband when they get married."

"So they paid guys to marry women back then?" Shad said.

"That's one way of putting it," Mrs. Reinhold said.

Shad narrowed his eyes beneath the hat. "And who's Katharina again?"

"Lilianna."

Shad pushed the hat back off of his forehead and looked at Lily, the Shifferdecker gleam in his eye. "You would *have* to pay somebody to marry *her*," he said.

"There will be none of that here, Mr. Shifferdecker," Mrs. Reinhold said, pointing her eyes at him.

Shad pulled the hat back down. Lily tried to will her face to stop going blotchy.

"So we have two things going on at the same time," Mrs. Reinhold said. "The suitors of Bianca are competing with each other, dressing up in disguises and pretending to be music teachers so they can be near her. And Petruchio is wooing Katharina."

"Wooing?" Shad said. "Does that mean what I think it means?"

"I doubt that," Mrs. Reinhold said. "In Petruchio's case, it means he has to 'tame' her, force her to say she'll marry him through whatever means possible—and Katharina gives him a run for his money, literally. There is much chasing around the room and so forth. It's a hilarious scene."

So there's no kissing or anything, right? Lily wanted to ask.

She even thought it was worth the snickers she was sure to get, and she was raising her hand when Mrs. Reinhold said, "It isn't your typical boy-meets-girl-and-proposes scene. You can trust me on that."

She went on to explain what the other scenes were about, but Lily didn't hear most of it. She was too busy trying to decide whether this was really worth it, just to be on stage and hear clapping and be important for a half hour or so. She hadn't signed the contract yet. There was still time to back out.

"Now, then," Mrs. Reinhold said, "I trust you have read your scripts, and I also trust that you found them somewhat difficult to understand."

"Ya think?" Gary said. It was another high-five opportunity.

"So that you will see how those words you're struggling with actually make sense when they are performed, I've asked two of our college theater students who will be working with us to demonstrate what I mean."

She nodded to the two people she'd been talking to earlier. The guy had a handsome face, but his dark hair was sort of disorganized, and he was wearing baggy shorts and sandals, even though it was November. The girl was as thin as Lily herself and had a braid all the way to her waist. The bracelets around her ankles jingled as she walked to the front of the room.

"This is Ed," Mrs. Reinhold said, "and this is Victoria. They will be working with Lilianna and Shad on their scene. However, the scene they are going to perform for you is from another of Shakespeare's plays so that they will not be influenced in their creative choices by what Ed and Victoria do."

"We'll be performing a piece from *A Midsummer Night's Dream*," Ed said — in a voice so deep and booming it seemed to vibrate the walls.

And then he and Victoria arranged themselves into poses in the front of the classroom, heads bowed. On some unseen cue, they suddenly came to life, bantering back and forth in language so strange and beautiful Lily felt as if she were being hypnotized by it. Their eyes glowed as Victoria chased Ed from one side of their stage to the other, now jumping on him piggy-back fashion, now holding onto his ankle as he dragged her behind him like a ball and chain. Lily didn't know *exactly* what was going on every second, but she understood enough to be enchanted by it and to burst into clapping when they were finished. The guys whistled through their teeth, and Fiona started a standing ovation.

"You see how delightful it can be?" Mrs. Reinhold said.

Yes! Lily thought. *I have to do this—no matter how evil Shad Shifferdecker is!*

When lunchtime was over, Lily couldn't wait to get to math class to tell Reni. They were working in groups that day, so they raced through the problems so she could fill her in.

"It's going to just be the *best*," Lily told her as she was winding up the story.

"Even though you gotta get chased around by Shad Shifferdecker?" Reni said.

"It totally does gross me out," Lily said. "But you know what? When I was watching Ed and Victoria, it wasn't like they were Ed and Victoria anymore—they were their characters. So—I'll just pretend Shad's really Petruchio."

Reni rolled her big brown eyes. "And I thought Shifferdecker was a weird name."

Just before the bell rang, Mr. Chester told them to go back to their desks. When Lily got to hers, there was a piece of folded-up paper on it. Couldn't be a Girlz-Gram—she'd been with Reni the whole period.

As she picked it up, Marcie McCleary leaned in from her desk behind Lily's, chains rattling.

"Ashley left it there," she said. "You guys aren't *friends*, are you?"

"Uh, no," Lily said.

"So why'd she leave you a note?" Marcie said.

Lily shrugged, but she was getting that uneasy feeling again. The note could be about only one thing.

"Aren't you gonna open it?" Marcie said, stretching even further across her desktop.

"Later," Lily said.

Marcie looked disappointed. She might be trying to turn into a gang chick, Lily thought, but she still acted like the same old Marcie. She loved to know everybody's business. Even as Lily tucked the note into her gaping-open backpack, Marcie said, "If you want to write her back, I'll deliver it for you."

"That's okay," Lily said.

When the bell finally rang, Lily made her way to the girl's restroom. There were a bunch of girls already in there, so she dove into a stall and shut the door. With shaky fingers, she pulled out Ashley's note.

I mean it, Robbins, she had written. *Keep your hands off of Shad!*

Chapter 6

When Lily got home that afternoon after Girlz Only, the house smelled like fried chicken, Lily's current favorite thing to eat. She made a beeline for the kitchen without even stopping to dump her backpack and found Mom mashing potatoes—her second favorite thing to eat.

"Are we having company?" Lily said.

Mom's brown-sugar ponytail jiggled as she turned around, mouth twitching into a smile. "Do we have to have company to have a decent meal around here?"

"Well," Lily said, cocking her head. "Yeah."

Mom chuckled. "Yeah, I guess you're right. I'm going all out in honor of you being chosen for the Shakespeare program."

Lily felt her mouth dropping open. "Really?"

"Yes, really. We're always making a big thing out of it when Joe's team makes the championship or Art gets high marks at a contest, but we don't celebrate *your* accomplishments—probably because they're usually"—her mouth twitched some more—"different."

Lily lifted the lid on one of the pots and stared. "Gravy too?"

"Don't get too excited—it's out of a jar. Go wash up. I'll have Joe set the table tonight since you're the guest of honor."

"He'll yell."

"So what else is new?"

Joe did yell about having to set the table, and when they all sat down to eat, he was still whining about having to find five sets of silverware that all matched.

"I don't get what the big deal is," he said.

"Your sister has entered the drama world," Dad said. "That is a big deal."

"Nah. Drama's for sissies."

"I did drama in high school and college," Dad said.

"Okay—so it's *mostly* for sissies."

"I gotta disagree with you, Joe," Art said. "The drama kids at the high school are a little wacky, but they're cool."

"The two college kids that are gonna work with us are cool," Lily said.

"They weren't wearing strange clothes and carrying around bizarre props?" Dad said.

"Is a big floppy hat with a feather a prop?" Lily said.

"Could be."

"Then, yeah, they were."

"See," Joe said.

"There is nothing wrong with being a little wacky," Mom said.

"As long as you have other people to be wacky with," Art said. "Then it becomes like a thing. It's the ones who just whack-out on their own that get labeled weird."

"I am completely confused," Dad said. "Could someone pass the gravy?"

After supper, Lily zipped through her homework so she could work on her lines. Even though Mrs. Reinhold had said they had until Monday to learn them and it was only Tuesday, she wanted to get them all done by tomorrow. It would be neat to impress Ed and Victoria, *and* she wanted to show Shad that she meant business.

But it turned out to be harder than she'd expected. In the first place, there were words she'd never heard before and that made her lines difficult to remember. What was a *swain*? And a *coxcomb*? And a *craven*?

Besides that, if she were going to learn all her lines and where they came in, she had to know Shad's — Petruchio's — too, and his had even harder words than hers. She could barely imagine Shad saying, "In sooth" and "No, not a whit." Between that and all the "thy's" and "tis's" it was enough to tangle a person's brain.

But I want to do this, Lily thought. *I can do it!*

After all, Mrs. Reinhold said it would be a challenge. Lily hunkered down over the script and went to work.

By lights-out time, she had half of them memorized, and after she'd written in her journal to God, she curled up and recited the lines for Otto in the dark. He sat up, blinking at her.

" 'No such jade as you, if me you mean!' " she said — with vigor.

Otto's ears perked up.

" 'Too light for such a swain as you to catch!' " she said. " 'And yet as heavy as my weight *should* be!' "

Otto stood up on the bed.

" 'Well taken, and like a buzzard!' " she cried.

Otto barked so loud, Lily had to put a pillow over him to shush him up before Mom and Dad heard him.

I guess it's a pretty good sign if I can get Otto excited, Lily thought. *But it would be nice to have somebody to study my lines with — like a person.*

She closed her eyes and prayed some more.

Please, God, help me learn all my lines and help me be amazing in this part.

Another thought struck her.

And please don't let Ashley clobber me.

The uneasy feeling oozed in again. That made it hard to get to sleep.

Lily was the first one of the Girlz at the bench the next morning, so she got out her script to learn a few more lines. She was struggling with "I chafe you if you tarry—let me go!" when she felt somebody looking over her shoulder. It was Deputy Dog.

"Got a big test today, Robbins?" she said.

Lily shook her head and told her about the program.

"You're gonna like this, Robbins," Deputy Dog said. "It's right down your alley."

"It's hard, though," Lily said. "I'm trying to learn my lines."

"Let's see how you're doing."

She took the script out of Lily's hand and squinted at it. " 'Good morrow, Kate,' " she read in a deep, loud voice, " 'for that's your name, I hear.' "

Lily stared at her.

" 'Well have you heard—' " Deputy Dog prompted.

"Oh, yeah— 'Well have you heard, but something hard of hearing. They call me Katharine that do talk of me.' "

They went through the rest of the lines to the place where Lily had stopped memorizing. By then, Kresha had appeared and was watching them, wide-eyed under her bangs.

"You're gonna be a smash, Robbins," Deputy Dog said, handing the script back to Lily.

"Thanks," Lily said. That was about all she could say. She was still stunned that Deputy Dog could read Shakespeare.

"I like that play," Kresha said when D.D. had gone to break up a group of boys who were playing keep-away with somebody's math book.

"You do?" Lily said.

Kresha nodded eagerly. "Do some more!"

"I don't know the rest of the lines yet," Lily said. "I need somebody to practice them with."

"I will do it!" Kresha said.

Lily looked at her doubtfully. She didn't want to hurt her feelings, but Kresha had enough trouble with *regular* words. Lily shifted her eyes around.

"You not think I can help," Kresha said.

"It's not that," Lily said.

Kresha gave her a hard look.

"Okay, it is that. This is a different kind of English, Kresha."

"I can learn different," she said.

Lily sighed and handed her the script. "Okay — start from here."

She pointed to a spot. Kresha studied it for a moment.

" 'O, let me see — th-e-e walk,' " Kresha read. She looked up. "What is *thee*?"

Lily wanted to groan. "It's the same as *you*," she said. "It's hard to explain."

Kresha folded her arms. "I can learn. You teach me."

I don't have time to teach you! Lily wanted to scream. But she took the script back and looked at the lines.

"Okay," she said, "maybe it'll help if you know the story."

She told Kresha what Mrs. Reinhold had told them about Katharina and Petruchio and Bianca and the rest of them — jazzing it up a little so Kresha would be sure to get it. Kresha listened as if Lily were telling her some kind of cool secret, and when she was finished, Kresha snatched the script back from her and said, "Now we read!"

I don't see what difference it's really gonna make, Lily thought.

But she pointed to the spot on the script and said, "Start here."

" 'No, not a whit. I find you passing gentle,' " Kresha read. She looked slyly at Lily. " 'Twas told me you were rough and coy and sullen.' " She gave Lily another evil grin.

"Yeah," Lily said. "Yeah, that's it." She hoped she didn't sound too surprised, but it was hard not to be. Kresha had read it better than Deputy Dog.

"Hey," somebody said.

Kresha and Lily looked up to see Chelsea standing there, upper lip curled and eyes in slits. She tossed her hair back with a shake of her head.

"You didn't answer Ashley's note," she said, looking straight at Lily.

"So?" Lily said. Her heart was pounding again. She could feel Kresha stiffening beside her.

"That's rude," Chelsea said. "Ashley thinks so too."

"What do you want me to say?" Lily said.

Chelsea rolled her eyes so hard they seemed to disappear up into her head. "You are so weird." She glanced at Kresha as if that included her too. "Ashley means what she says: keep your hands off Shad."

"Why would I want to touch him anyway?" Lily said.

"Duh! You're doing a play together, as boyfriend and girlfriend," Chelsea said. "I know you don't know anything *about* boyfriends and girlfriends, but they *do*, like, hold hands and stuff."

It was Lily's turn to roll *her* eyes. "That just shows what you know about Shakespeare," she said.

"Who's Shakespeare?" Chelsea said. "He's not your boyfriend, is he?"

Kresha spat a laugh on Lily's arm. Chelsea glared at her.

"He wrote the scene we're doing," Lily said. "It's not about boyfriend and girlfriend—it's about this guy who wants to marry this girl, only she hates his guts."

"Well, that sounds lame," Chelsea said. She seemed to ponder it for a moment before she shook her hair back again. "You just better watch it," she said. "Ashley *can* be mean when she gets mad—and you're making her mad."

"So?" Lily said.

"So — why don't you just tell Mrs. Reinhold you want to do a different kind of scene? You're her little pet — she'll do whatever you want because you kiss up to her all the time."

"I do not!" Lily said. And then she stopped herself. She'd learned a long time ago it wasn't a good thing to try to defend yourself in an argument with Chelsea or Ashley. They were experts at turning things around so she ended up looking blotchy and feeling like a moron.

"That's the scene we're gonna do," Lily said. "Ashley just needs to — to get a life."

She looked at Kresha, who was nodding furiously. That made her feel stronger.

"Did you just say Ashley needs to get a life?" Chelsea said, eyes popping.

"Yeah," Lily said.

"And you really want me to tell her you *said* that?"

"Yeah," Lily said.

Chelsea slowly shook her head. "You are in *so* much trouble," she said.

And then she made a quick little turn and strutted off — as if she couldn't wait to find Ashley and start the "trouble" without delay.

It wasn't until she was gone that Lily realized Suzy and Zooey were huddled together by the water fountain.

"You hear that?" Kresha said to them, hands planted indignantly on her hips.

"Yes!" Zooey said. "Lily — I'm so scared for you!"

Suzy could only give a white-faced nod.

Lily was a little scared herself, but Kresha put up her hand.

"No!" she said.

"No what?" Zooey said.

"No be scared of that girl — or that Ashley girl."

49

"You heard her!" Zooey said.

"No," Kresha said, folding her arms across her chest. "We will—what is word—pro—what is word when you take care—"

"Protect?" Suzy said.

"Ya!" Kresha snapped her finger. "We will protect Lily from those girls."

"Us?" Zooey said.

"Ya—us!" Kresha flung her arm around Lily's shoulder. "We love Lily. We not let nobody hurt her. We will protect her."

Zooey began to nod—slowly, but she was nodding. Suzy still looked as if she'd just been stricken with laryngitis.

"You would really do that for me?" Lily said.

"Yes," Kresha and Zooey said together.

Suzy gave an anxious nod.

Lily looked at the cowering Suzy and the bug-eyed Zooey and the feisty but skinny Kresha. They were a ragged little bunch of bodyguards—but they cared. It was a good feeling that took the place of the uneasiness in her stomach.

"You guys are the best," Lily said.

As they all put their hands together to seal the promise, she added to herself, *Wow! That prayer got answered fast.*

Chapter 7

In English class, Lily asked Mrs. Reinhold if she could study her lines when she was finished with the day's assignment.

Mrs. Reinhold almost smiled. "I knew you would give this 550 percent, Lilianna."

"Thanks," Lily said. She didn't add, *I sure hope Shad does the same thing.*

There wasn't much chance of that, as far as Lily was concerned. All the more reason to be perfect in the scene in case she was the only one of the two of them who could make it wonderful.

Lily raced through the vocabulary assignment, and then pulled her script out of the top of her backpack. She still hadn't gotten the zipper fixed, but at least that made it easy to locate the script whenever she had a minute.

She smoothed it out on her desk, closed her eyes, and began to whisper the lines she knew already.

"'Well aim'd of such a young one.' Petruchio replies, 'Now, by Saint George, I am too young for you.'"

"Robbins!" Lily heard someone else whisper.

She looked up to see Ashley glaring from the seat in front of her.

"What?" Lily whispered back.

"You're all hissing—I can't concentrate."

Lily glanced warily around for Mrs. Reinhold—who allowed *no* talking while they were working—but she was standing in the doorway chatting with another teacher.

"I'm studying my lines," Lily whispered.

The minute the words were out of her mouth, she wanted to bite them back. Ashley's eyes went down into mean little slits.

"Don't bother," she said to Lily. "You are *so* not doing that scene."

"Yes, I am," Lily said, and then she set the script up in front of her.

When Ashley had flounced herself back around, Lily did sneak a peek over at Suzy. She was watching, face ashen.

She's really gonna protect me, Lily thought.

But as Lily returned to her lines, another thought occurred to her. What was Ashley really going to do, besides just hassle her? Ashley was mean-mouthed, but Lily had never heard of her actually hitting anybody. Just in case, though, Lily whispered a quick prayer.

Right before the bell was supposed to ring, Mrs. Reinhold told them all to pass their vocabulary papers forward. Lily stuffed her script into the top of her backpack and turned around to get the papers coming up the row.

"Hurry up, Robbins," Ashley said. "Don't make a career out of collecting the stupid things."

Lily just smiled to herself. If that was as bad as it got, what was she worried about?

The next period, the class had a geography test that took up the whole hour, so Lily didn't have any more time to study her lines. Still, she had almost all of them; that was probably enough to impress Ed and Victoria and give Shad a clue. But she kept running the words in her head until they began to sound like a song in her mind.

When the lunch bell finally rang, Lily took off for Mrs. Reinhold's room, grinning to herself. This was going to be so awesome.

Mrs. Reinhold started the rehearsal with an announcement.

"When we perform these scenes," she said to the group, "we will need to have a way to pull them all together — a theme, so to speak — or a bridging system."

Lily had no idea what she was talking about, and from the looks on everybody else's faces, they were as confused as she was.

"For instance," Mrs. Reinhold said, "we could set our stage up like a classroom with a 'teacher' explaining *Shrew* to the class, and as she approaches a particular scene, the actors get up and perform it."

Nobody said anything. Shad pretended to be snoring.

Yikes, Lily thought, *that does sound boring.*

Natalie raised her hand. "Do we *have* to do it that way?" she said.

Shad snored even louder, and Gary joined him. Mrs. Reinhold hushed them both with a look.

"No," she said. "But if you do not want to do it that way, you will have to come up with ideas of your own. Think about it, and on Monday we will brainstorm as a group." She paused. "I think we will hear people run their lines from memory first that day so that we all have a sense of the various scenes before we determine how to link them together."

Lily's hand popped up. "So — on Monday it's like we're performing almost."

"Not even close," Ed said. "We've got a long way to go." Then he glanced at Mrs. Reinhold, as if to say, *So would you hurry it up, lady?*

"All right, then," Mrs. Reinhold said.

She went on to introduce the two other scenes to their college directors. Ed and Victoria hurried over to Shad and Lily and started pushing desks around.

"Mrs. Reinhold hates it when people move her stuff," Lily said.

"This isn't a classroom right now," Ed said in his big, booming voice. "It's a studio — and we have work to do."

Studio. Lily liked that word. She quickly helped Ed and Victoria put four chairs in a huddle, while Shad tried to talk Mrs. Reinhold into letting him wear the hat again.

"Not until you can spell Shakespeare," Mrs. Reinhold said.

You'll never see that hat again, Petruchio, Lily thought.

"Okay, you two," Victoria said, bracelets jangling up her arm. "Get out your scripts and let's do a read-through."

Shad gave her a blank look.

"Your script, pal," Ed said. "Do you have it?"

"Oh, yeah," Shad said. Then he reached into the back pocket of his too-big khakis and fished out a folded-up square. It looked like he hadn't opened it since yesterday.

"Do you have yours, Lily?" Victoria said.

"Yes," Lily said, "but could I try the first part of it from memory?"

Victoria's eyebrows went up. "You've learned some of your lines already?"

Lily nodded and tried not to look too smug. If Shad was catching any of it, she couldn't tell. He was scowling at his script as if he'd never seen it before.

"All right, let's give it a try," Ed boomed. "Don't worry too much about inflection this first time through —"

"What's inflection?" Shad said. "You mean, like an earache?"

Lily rolled her eyes. She didn't know what *inflection* was either, but she knew it wasn't that.

"Not *infection,*" Victoria said patiently. "*Inflection* — it's what you do with your voice to give it expression. For now, we're just reading through to make sure you understand everything you're saying and can pronounce the words correctly."

Lily nodded. Shad slouched down in the desk and propped the script in front of him like a barrier. This wasn't looking good.

"You start us off, Shad," Ed said.

"Can you call me Petruchio?" Shad said.

"Sure." Ed poked at Shad's shoe with his foot. "Go for it, Petruchio."

Shad sighed and squinted his eyes at the script. " 'Good morning, Kate, for that's your name, I hear.' "

"Not 'morning,' " Victoria said. " 'Morrow.' Go ahead, Lily."

"Uh— 'Well have you heard but something hard of hearing. They call me Katharine that do talk of me.' "

Lily sighed. Victoria gave her an approving nod and looked at Shad.

"Oh— me again?" Shad said. " 'You lie, in faith; for you are called plain Kate, and bonny Kate, and sometimes Kate the curst—' " Shad looked up. "I like that, Kate the curst." He gave Lily an evil grin and went on. " 'But Kate, the prettiest Kate in' —where?"

"Christendom," Victoria said. "It means all the Christian countries."

"Oh," Shad said. He looked at Lily again. "I don't know about *that*."

"You don't get it, pal," Ed said. "Kate isn't that good-looking. Petruchio's just laying it on thick to get her to marry him so he can get her father's money."

Lily felt a little blotchy, but she reminded herself that Ed was talking about Kate, not Lily. She wished Shad would get on with it or she was going to forget her next line. *It didn't take Shakespeare this long to* write *it,* she thought.

" 'Kate of Kate Hall,' " Shad droned on. " 'My super-dainty Kate—' " Another doubtful look at Lily. " 'For dainties are all cates' —what's a *cate*?"

"Some kind of dainty little tidbit," Victoria said.

"What's a tidbit?"

"You don't get out much, do you, pal?" Ed said, grinning.

Lily wasn't grinning. It was all she could do not to take Shad by the arm and shake him.

"'And, therefore, Kate, take this of me, Kate of my con-so-la-tion'—whatever that is—'Hearing thy mildness praised in every town'—yeah, right—'thy virtues spoke of, and thy beauty sounded'—Dude, this guy wants the money *bad*—'yet not so deeply as to thee belongs—'" Shad gave a huge sigh, as if he'd just done an hour of hard labor. "'Myself am moved to woo thee for my wife.'"

There was silence. Ed and Victoria looked at Lily.

"Oh!" Lily said. "Um—"

Shad had taken so long, she *did* forget her next line.

"You can look at your script," Victoria said.

"No, I've got it," Lily said. "Uh—'Moved! Let him that moved you hither *remove* you hence. I knew at the first you were a moveable.'"

"What's a moveable?" Shad said.

Victoria and Ed both laughed.

"What?" Shad said.

"That's your next line," Ed said. "Almost—look at it."

Shad read, "'Why, what's a moveable?' Cool!"

"You won't forget that one," Victoria said. "Lily?"

But Lily's mind was blank. With all the stuff going on while Shad read his part, she couldn't remember a single thing she'd memorized.

"Why don't you just get your script out?" Victoria said.

"I had all these lines before I came in here," Lily said, glaring at Shad.

"It's okay—just get your script."

Lily shot one more dagger look at Shad before she reached for her backpack. *Is there anything in my life you can't ruin, Shad Shiffer-decker?* she thought as she felt around for her script. *Come on, where is it?*

It wasn't where she'd left it, right on top. Feeling her face blotching and going straight to bright red, she yanked out the books and binders and peered into the backpack. The script was gone.

"Can't you find it?" Victoria said.

Her voice was no longer patient. She was, in fact, fiddling with her braid and giving Ed looks that said, *We've got ourselves a couple of winners here.*

"I had it at the end of third period!" Lily said.

"Maybe it fell out," Ed said. "Go ask Mrs. Reinhold for another one."

Lily felt as if her heart had stopped. "I can't tell Mrs. Reinhold I lost my script!"

"Oh, for Pete's sake, what's she gonna do?" Victoria said. "Take away your birthday?"

Ed was a little kinder. "Just go ask her," he said. "We got work to do, girlfriend."

Lily felt like a piece of lead as she dragged herself out of her desk and over to Mrs. Reinhold, next to Wesley and Hilary's group. She was smiling and nodding as if all was going superbly. The smiling and the nodding both stopped when Lily said, "I've lost my script. Could I please have another one?"

"You've only had it twenty-four hours, Lilianna," Mrs. Reinhold said. "How did you manage to lose it already?"

"I—"

"Never mind," Mrs. Reinhold said. "There is an extra copy on my desk. I made one for Shad, expecting *him* to be the one who would need it—not you."

"I'm sorry," Lily mumbled.

As she hurried up to Mrs. Reinhold's desk, she heard Wesley and Hilary's college girl say to them, "Keeping track of your script is part of the acting discipline."

It made Lily want to throw herself down and cry—but she was pretty sure that *wasn't* part of the acting discipline. Instead, she picked up the extra script and made a vow to herself: *I will have all my lines memorized by tomorrow, and I'll be able to say them no matter how much Shad messes up.*

It was a lot to vow. She added a prayer on her way back to her group: *God, help me with this, would you? I want it so bad.*

She was glum that afternoon at Girlz Only Club as she told the Girlz.

"How could you lose your script?" Reni said. "You have it in your hand most of the time."

"You know the lines, Lily," Kresha said, her face stormy. "You know *all* the lines. That Shad is evil!"

"Oh, ya think?" Lily said. "If it wasn't wrong to hate—I would *so* hate him."

"Do you want us to help you find your old script, Lily?" Zooey said. "So you can show Mrs. Reinhold you aren't a loser?"

"Don't bother," Suzy said.

It was the first thing she'd said since the meeting started. Lily thought she looked whiter than usual.

"What do you mean?" Reni said. "Why shouldn't she bother?"

"Because I don't think she lost it," Suzy said. Lily could see her swallowing as if she had a mouthful of peanut butter. "I think I saw Ashley take something out of the top of your backpack when we were passing the papers in third period."

"Why didn't you say something before?" Reni said.

Suzy seemed to sink further into the yellow beanbag chair as if she wanted it to swallow her up.

"Well, duh!" Zooey said. "What good would it do? You really think Suzy's gonna tell on Ashley?"

"Besides, I'm not even sure," Suzy said. "There was a lot going on right then, and I couldn't see everything she did."

"Do you sit there and watch everything that goes on?" Reni said to Suzy.

"We're supposed to be protecting Lily, aren't we?" she said in a meek little voice.

"We are?" Reni said.

"You missed it this morning," Zooey said.

While she filled Reni in, Lily went over to sit by Suzy.

"It's really okay, Suzy," Lily said. "But thanks for trying."

"We must try hard more!" Kresha said.

"I don't see why," Reni said. "Even if we see Ashley do something, we're too scared to tell on her."

"But Ashley doesn't beat people up," Lily said.

"No," Reni said, "she just steals from them. Now, if she had, like, threatened to break my hand so I couldn't play the violin, that would be worth telling somebody — but you got another script, so what's the big deal?"

It got very quiet in the basement. *Reni's doing it again,* Lily thought. *She thinks her thing is more important than mine.*

"Ouch, Reni," Zooey finally said. "I think you hurt Lily's feelings."

But Lily tilted her chin up and looked straight at Reni. "No. I'm fine. I don't need any protection. I'll just do this on my own."

Suzy looked miserably from Lily to Reni. Zooey picked up the plate of oatmeal cookies and said, "Is it snack time yet?"

There wasn't much more to talk about, and the Girlz broke up early. Reni had to rush off to a violin lesson her mom was picking her up for, so Lily started for home alone. She'd only gone a few steps away from Zooey's house when she heard Kresha calling her from behind.

"Lily!" she said. "You want help?"

Lily stopped and shook her head as Kresha ran up to her, hair flying and socks falling down.

"I don't think I really need protecting," Lily said.

"No," Kresha said. "Help with the play."

"You mean, help me with my lines?"

Kresha nodded happily. "Like this morning."

Lily thought about it a second, then she said, "Why don't you come home with me now?"

Kresha grinned and slung her arm around Lily's shoulder as they started to walk. It made Lily feel a lot better.

Chapter 8

For the next two days, Lily studied her script at every possible moment—when she was in the bathtub, while she was loading the dishwasher, whenever she had to go anyplace in the van. Joe claimed it was driving him crazy. Art told him he didn't have that far to go anyway.

Kresha practiced with Lily after Girlz Club and before school and sometimes even on the phone. A couple of times, Dad went over the lines with her too.

"My hat is off to Mrs. Reinhold," he said Thursday night when they were running over them in his study. "This scene can be a little racy, depending on how you interpret it, but she has skillfully taken out anything that could be considered bawdy."

"Huh?" Lily said.

"She cleaned it up so that only the really fun stuff is left."

"Oh," Lily said.

It definitely seemed like it was fun for Kresha. She got better and better at saying Petruchio's lines with expression, even with her cute little accent, and sometimes she could hardly keep from laughing when Lily said Kate's lines.

"Am I supposed to be funny?" Lily said to her Friday morning when they were practicing on the bench.

"Ya!" Kresha said. "You look so—" She pulled her face into an angry frown. "He will smile—you will frown. That makes me laugh."

"Oh," Lily said, "I get it."

"Are you guys done yet?" Zooey said.

She and Suzy were sitting on the ground, leaning against the brick wall, listening. Although Lily would have loved to do the scene one more time, just to be *sure* she was ready for lunchtime, Lily took the script from Kresha and tucked it into the bottom of her backpack. They looked so left out sitting over there. She knew she would hate to feel like that.

"You're done?" Zooey said.

"Yeah," Lily said.

"Yea!" Zooey said.

She scrambled up and dug into her bag, pulling out a disposable camera.

"Okay—everybody on the bench—I gotta take a picture."

"Reni's not here," Suzy said.

"She's never here in the morning," Zooey said. "This picture is for the page about us meeting at the bench in the morning."

"What page?" Lily said.

Zooey rolled her eyes as if they were all being incredibly dumb.

"In the scrapbook," she said. "Remember, I told you I was making one?"

"Oh!" Lily said. "Okay—how do you want us, Zooey? We'll pose."

That brought a smile to Zooey's face, and it made Lily feel better as well. Suzy, however, still looked a little forlorn.

Two things surprised Lily over those two days. One was that Deputy Dog stopped by each morning to see how the scene was coming along. She always chuckled and nodded like she was really at a play.

The other thing was that although Ashley continued to give her black looks every time she got the chance, especially in the mornings when she passed them at the bench, she didn't leave any more notes or make any more threats—or rip off any more of Lily's stuff. Lily decided she'd been right: Ashley might talk big, but she was harmless.

The thing that didn't surprise her was that Shad didn't seem to be learning his lines—at all. He astonished everyone by passing the how-to-spell-Shakespeare quiz, and he was reading the script a little better—he said it was wearing the hat that helped—but he showed no signs of even starting to commit it to memory. Lily was getting nervous.

On Friday at lunchtime rehearsal, Ed and Victoria looked a little nervous too. Victoria was constantly fidgeting with her braid, and Ed kept calling Shad "Pal" every other word. It was all apparently lost on Shad.

"You know you have to have these by Monday, Pal," Ed said.

"Yeah," Shad said.

"Have you even started trying to learn them?" Victoria said.

Shad didn't answer. He just looked at them as if they were expecting him to memorize the whole Constitution.

While Shad continued to chew on a toothpick, Ed and Victoria put their heads together and whispered. This *really* didn't look good.

"Okay," Ed said, "Victoria and I are gonna show you two some of the blocking we've got planned for this scene. Then maybe you'll see how important it is to have the lines down pat so you don't even have to think about them while you're doing all this stuff."

"Your lines will be delivered differently because you're totally different people," Victoria said. "This is just for blocking."

"What's blocking?" Lily said, pencil poised to write it down.

"It's the movement," Victoria said. "You aren't going to just stand there and say your lines to each other. The fun of the scene is in the action."

By now, Ed had cleared out a little space and set up two chairs side by side. "This is the couch," he said, pointing to them.

"Got it," Shad said.

Victoria stood on one side of the playing space, arms folded and foot tapping, as if she were *very* ticked off. Ed came in from the other side, stood, and gave her back an evil grin.

" 'Good morrow, Kate!' " he said in his booming voice.

From that moment on, Lily was enchanted. Ed and Victoria turned into Kate and Petruchio and chased each other, tumbled on the floor, and did somersaults over the couch as they bantered back and forth with the lines. At one point, Victoria was standing up on the "couch" while Ed circled her—and then when he said one particularly fake-mushy line, Victoria jumped right on his back and pummeled his chest with her fists, while he went on raving about her beauty. Lily laughed so hard she had tears in her eyes. Shad was almost on the floor, cackling like a chicken.

When Ed and Victoria were done—and out of breath—they both stood in front of Lily and Shad.

"You see how cool this is gonna be?" Ed said to Shad.

"Yeah!" he said. "Can we try some of that?"

"No," Victoria said, "not until you learn the lines. We do nothing— nada—until you have every word memorized."

Lily's heart sank. All through the scene she had been able to *see* herself up there, standing on the chair, fuming at Petruchio while the audience roared. But could Shad learn all those lines by Monday when he hadn't even started?

She didn't even have to ask what would happen if Shad *didn't* come through. It was in the contract: Mrs. Reinhold would cut the scene.

It's not fair, she thought. *It's just not fair.*

It was almost time for the bell to ring, and most of the kids were already hurrying on to their fifth-period classes. Lily was slow getting it together; the pure sadness of it all was dragging her down.

All the college kids left, except for Victoria and Ed. They were in the corner with Mrs. Reinhold, talking in low, adult voices. Lily couldn't really hear them, and she didn't try. She didn't want to hear them tell Mrs. R that Shad and Lily's scene was hopeless.

She was almost to the door, however, when one sentence did drift up above the others, and she couldn't help hearing it.

"Shad has dyslexia," Mrs. Reinhold said. "That accounts for a lot of it."

Lily felt strangely cold as she slipped out of the room. Shad had a disease? Was that why he acted like such a goofball all the time?

Wow! she thought. *Maybe Mrs. Reinhold is letting him do this because she feels sorry for him or something.*

It bugged her all afternoon, and by that evening, she decided she had to at least find out what dyslexia was. It was family night, but Art had to play in the pep band at a basketball game, so it was just Mom, Dad, Lily, and Joe. Lily didn't always like it that much when Art wasn't there to fend off some of Joe's comments, but that night, Mom gave Joe some medicine for a cold he'd caught, and he was snoozing loudly by the time the pizza arrived. So Lily settled into the family room with Mom and Dad to herself.

"Dad?" she said as she pulled the pepperonis off of a slice of pizza and stacked them up like coins.

"Yes, Lilliputian," Dad said. His eyes were sparkly behind his glasses. On family night, he always put C. S. Lewis aside and focused on the kids.

"Do you know anything about a disease called dyslexia?"

She could see Mom's mouth twitching.

"What?" Lily said.

"It's not exactly a disease," Dad said. "It's a learning disability. Your mother probably knows more about it than I do."

"You don't have it, do you, Mom?" Lily said.

Mom actually laughed. "No, Lil—but I teach kids with dyslexia all the time. Something has gone wrong in the person's brain, and, to put it simply, he sees words backwards. It makes learning to read a real chore, and a lot of times, dyslexics are either labeled as 'slow' or they become behavior problems."

"Oh," Lily said. "No wonder."

She popped the stack of pepperonis into her mouth.

"That's it?" Mom said.

Lily nodded. It made a lot of sense now. But it didn't make anything better. In fact, it probably made things worse, and she didn't want to talk about it.

"So," Dad said, as he put his stack of pepperonis on Lily's plate. "What else is on your mind these days?"

"You might as well take advantage of being the only kid here," Mom said.

That was true, Lily decided. So she told Mom and Dad about Zooey and Suzy—how left out they were feeling. And about Reni, who thought violin was the only thing that was important anymore. By the time she was finished describing all that, Dad had eaten two more pieces of pizza.

"That's a lot to deal with, Lil," Mom said. "What's God saying about it?"

"What's he saying?" Lily said. "I don't know—I don't ever hear anything." She swallowed a wad of pepperoni. "Am I supposed to?"

"Are you listening?" Dad said.

Lily gave them a look that made Mom's mouth twitch. "I'm sure you tell God plenty," Mom said. "Just be sure you listen to what *he* has to say too."

"Listening's not the best thing that I do," Lily said.

Dad chuckled. "But you're getting better, Lilliputian. Hang in there."

Lily really did try to listen that night when she was writing to God in her journal. Just as always, no vision appeared in her bedroom. She'd always thought it would be so much simpler for everybody if God worked like that. But she did get an idea.

If she was praying for Suzy and Zooey and Reni and Kresha—
maybe she ought to be praying for Shad too. After all, he did have that
learning thing.

She had to admit it was hard to mention Shad's name to God—and
even harder to ask for good things for him, instead of hoping he'd just
drop off the face of the earth. But she did it.

Just, please, God, she thought as she snuggled in with Otto, *let it all
work. I want it so bad.*

Chapter 9

Kresha came over several times that weekend, and by the time Sunday night came, Lily was word perfect. In fact, they could *both* run the whole scene without the script.

"I wish *you* were playing Petruchio," Lily said to her. "Then my problems would be over."

Monday morning, Lily went to her locker when she got to school, and she was just closing it up when she saw Shad walk by at the end of the row. Lily wanted to run after him and ask him if he'd learned his lines, but of course she didn't. Even if he *had*—which would be a miracle—he sure wasn't going to tell *her*.

She hiked her backpack over her shoulder and headed for the hall. She was just rounding the corner of the bank of lockers when out of the corner of her eye, she saw Shad, standing at the top of the stairs. Ashley was with him.

Lily backed up so they wouldn't see her and peeked around the corner. Ashley was standing in front of Shad, who had his back to Lily, and she was obviously chewing him out.

What do I need a boyfriend for? Lily thought. *I can fight with Joe at home.*

From behind Shad, Lily could see something white sticking out of his back pocket. It looked like his script. She hoped he'd had it *out* of that pocket since Friday.

And then as if she had read Lily's mind, Ashley suddenly reached behind Shad and snatched the paper out.

"Hey!" Lily heard Shad yell. "That's my script! I'll get busted if I don't have it!"

Ashley held it behind her back and smiled coyly up at Shad, shaking her head.

"Come on, Ash," Shad said. "I gotta have that, man."

He made a lunge for Ashley, but she dodged him and ran in the other direction. Shad caught her by the arm, amid shrieks of laughter from Ashley, who was still clutching the script.

She acts like that's funny, Lily thought. *Yikes!*

Just then, Ashley let out a particularly shrill shriek as Shad twirled her around and got her in an armlock. Art had done that enough times to Lily for her to know Ashley wasn't getting out of that anytime soon.

Get the script back from her, Shad, Lily wanted to yell. *Forget her— get the script!*

Shad did try, but Ashley managed to let go of it with a flick of the wrist—which was the only part of her that was free. Pages scattered everywhere like big pieces of confetti.

No! Lily almost screamed. It was all she could do not to run after it and snatch up all the pages before they were lost forever under people's feet.

And then Deputy Dog appeared out of nowhere, thumbs hooked over her belt.

Shad had by then let go of Ashley and was trying to collect the pages of his script. Ashley had to lean against the stair rail, she was so hysterical with laughter.

Lily watched Deputy Dog and held her breath.

"I'm pickin' up this stuff she threw all over," Shad said. "She's a litterbug."

He's okay so far, Lily thought. *At least he's not making smart remarks.*

"You two weren't carrying on up here, were you?" Deputy Dog said.

"Nah," Shad said.

Ashley didn't say anything. She was still laughing into her hand.

I'd be dying, Lily thought. *They'd have to take me to the hospital!*

Deputy Dog looked at both of them, and then she went slowly over to Ashley. "You think it's funny now," she said to her. "But if I catch the two of you all over each other, you're going down. Are we clear on that?"

Ashley nodded. Her face was so red from holding back laughter that Lily felt sure she would explode any minute. It was hard not to wish she would.

"I don't believe I heard an answer," Deputy Dog said, cupping her hand around her ear.

"Yes!" Ashley said. When Deputy Dog turned back to Shad, she made a face behind her back.

Turn around now, D.D.! Lily wanted to call out.

But Deputy Dog was concentrating on Shad.

"What is this you're trying to salvage anyway?" she said, nodding to the pages Shad now held in a wad.

"This scene I gotta do," Shad said.

"What kind of scene?"

Shad shrugged. "Just some Shakespeare thing."

It was the first time Lily had ever seen Deputy Dog look surprised. "You're in that special program?" she said.

"Yeah," Shad said. "I guess."

"Well, if you intend to *stay* in it, I suggest you steer clear of your girlfriend here, or you're going to get yourself suspended."

"Yeah, I know," Shad said.

"Yeah, well, it's one thing to know and another to act on it."

"I got it," Shad said. "Can I go now?"

Deputy Dog nodded, and Shad took off like a shot down the stairs. Ashley at least had the good sense to wait until Deputy Dog had moved down the hall the other way before she charged after him.

Get a clue! Lily thought.

But as Ashley disappeared, Lily sagged against the lockers. In spite of all her prayers, it didn't look like there was much hope of getting to do the scene. Shad's script was now all torn up. Ashley was obviously still after him to quit. And if he stayed out of trouble for two more weeks, it was going to be the miracle of the millennium.

She was in a sour mood the rest of the morning. Even Ashley's curled lip in third period couldn't make it worse. When Lily arrived at lunchtime rehearsal, she sank into her desk and looked miserably around the room.

I might as well take everything in, she thought. *Because this is probably my last day doing this.*

Everyone had scripts out, and the groups were whispering their lines to each other when Mrs. Reinhold called them to order. Shad arrived about then, and Ed took him aside in the back corner. Mrs. Reinhold called on Wesley and Hilary to run their lines in front of the group first.

Probably because she knows they're gonna be perfect, Lily thought.

"Are you set, Lily?" Victoria whispered to her.

Lily nodded. Victoria patted her hand, and they both focused on the front, where Wesley and Hilary were taking their places as Lucentio and Bianca.

"Don't worry too much about expression," Mrs. Reinhold said. "We just want to see if you know the lines."

70

It turned out that they did—sort of. They stumbled several times and had to have Judith, one of their college coaches, prompt them. When they were finished, everyone clapped half-heartedly, but Mrs. Reinhold didn't exactly look overwhelmed.

"It's going to have to be much smoother than that," she said. "Don't begin blocking until you're more sure of the lines." She pursed her lips for a second. "We have less than two weeks now, people."

At least they're still in it, Lily thought. *Why couldn't she let me work with Wesley?*

"Lilianna and Mr. Shifferdecker," Mrs. Reinhold said. "Let's hear yours now."

Lily turned around to see Ed and Shad high-fiving each other. Shad got up and took a leisurely stroll up to the front. Lily followed. She felt like she was going to her own funeral.

They stood together at the front of the room, and everybody got quiet. Shad turned to Lily and gave her his evil smile.

You think this is funny! Lily thought. *You want me to look like a moron in front of people. I think I hate—*

She stopped herself. *Sorry, God,* she prayed quickly. *Just help him get at least a little of it, okay?*

"Go," Ed said.

Shad smiled at Lily once more and said, " 'Good morrow, Kate, for that's your name, I hear.' "

Lily tried not to drop her teeth. She managed to say her line, and then Shad launched into his long speech. His eyes were sparkling, and he was grinning and half-laughing as he teased her with the words.

And he didn't miss one.

Lily was glad it was a long speech. That gave her time to recover from her shock and recall her own line.

The minute she said it, Shad was back with his, for all the world as if he were enjoying every minute of it. Lily started to too. She was only

71

half-aware that the rest of the group was laughing. It was as if she and Shad were having a real conversation.

Shad started to mess up once, but the second Ed said, " 'Come, come, you wasp—' " Shad was off again, delivering the lines as if he'd made them up himself. The more into it he got, the more Lily did. When he crowed out, " 'Will you, nill you, I will marry you,' " the room exploded into applause.

Lily could only stare, open-mouthed. Shad, however, did several elaborate bows until Ed had to drag him back to his seat.

"Well, now," Mrs. Reinhold said. "That's the way Shakespeare should be done. That sets the standard for everyone."

The group didn't look quite as happy about that, but Lily didn't care. Maybe this was going to happen after all.

The last group did its scene, trying hard to live up to Shad and Lily's "standard." As soon as they were finished, Wesley and Hilary got out their scripts and started studying madly. But Mrs. Reinhold called everyone together. It was time to brainstorm about a tie-together theme.

She stood at the chalkboard, chalk in hand, and raised her eyebrows. The students all looked at each other.

"Any ideas?" Mrs. Reinhold said. "I asked you to be thinking about this."

"I forgot about it," Philip said. "I was too busy trying to learn my lines."

"Not a problem," Mrs. Reinhold said. "We can always go with my classroom idea."

There was a low moan. Lily put her hand up.

"Lilianna?" Mrs. R said.

"I thought of one way," Lily said. "We could have two kids in a time capsule and they get stuck in Shakespeare's time, and they eavesdrop on all these scenes."

"La-ame," Shad said.

"Really?" Mrs. Reinhold said. "Let's hear your idea, Shad."

"I ain't got one," Shad said.

"Then I suggest you withhold judgment on other people's contributions. Anyone else?"

"Who's gonna be in the time capsule, though?" Fiona said, looking at Lily.

"I can recruit two more students from the eighth-grade class," Mrs. Reinhold said. "Their lines would be in modern English, so it shouldn't be a problem."

"I just think it sounds childish," Natalie said. "No offense—what's your name?"

"Lily," Lily said. No offense? How wasn't she supposed to take offense at being called childish?

"It's all in how you portray it," Mrs. Reinhold said. "It sounds like the best idea so far."

"It's the *only* idea!" Hilary said.

"Precisely," Mrs. Reinhold said.

"Could you give us some more time to think about it?" Natalie said.

"No," Mrs. Reinhold said. "There is no more time. We have to get started on this part of the production right away—this afternoon."

"Aw, man," Gary said.

"What does that mean, Mr. Quincy?"

"I just don't want to look stupid up there."

"Then don't," Mrs. Reinhold said. She tapped her chalk on the board. "Unless I hear some other ideas, we will use Lilianna's."

"Going once," Ed said. "Going twice—"

Nobody would look up.

"Sold!" Ed said.

"Way to go, Lily," Victoria whispered to her.

Lily could feel the disgusted eyes of the rest of the kids looking at her. And it wasn't just their eyes. When the bell rang, Lily couldn't pick up her backpack fast enough. She was in such a hurry, she lifted it sideways—and all the contents dumped themselves out of the broken zipper and onto the floor.

Give me a break, somebody! Lily thought. With a sigh she got down on all fours behind the desks to collect her stuff. Beyond her the other kids began to file out.

"Is that Lily girl gone?" she heard Natalie say.

"Yeah," Wesley said. "I'd be outta here too, if I'd brought up a stupid idea like hers."

Lily tried to make herself small.

"We are *so* going to look like morons," Natalie said. "She's a good actress, but she's so *weird.*"

Their conversation trailed out the door. Lily sat on the floor and fought back the tears.

Chapter 10

In spite of all the good things that had happened during rehearsal, Lily flopped down on her bed late that afternoon, after going to Girlz Club and running lines with Kresha, and moaned into the pillow.

Otto jumped up beside her, his rope toy hanging out of his mouth like a rag.

"I don't want to play right now, Otto," Lily said. "I've had the *worst* day!"

Otto contented himself with chewing the rope, but he kept his eyes rolled up toward Lily.

"I want to be unique," Lily wailed to him. "I want to know what makes me special—you know, like, what my thing is. But I hate being called weird."

"It's pretty weird when you sit around talking to yourself," Art said from the doorway.

Lily didn't even have the energy to throw a pillow at him.

"I was talking to Otto," she said.

"That's just about as weird."

"Call me anything else, but don't call me that."

"Don't have a coronary," Art said.

"Could you close my door on your way out?" Lily said.

Art glanced out into the hall, then came into the room, and shut the door. "We gotta talk," he said.

He perched himself on the far corner of Lily's bed, and Otto growled.

"Relax, mutt," Art said. "I don't want your gross toy."

"You wanna talk to *me*?" Lily said.

"Yeah. Is it just me, or do Mom and Dad act like they're up to something?"

"What do you mean?" Lily said. She been so wrapped up in her lines, she'd barely noticed Mom and Dad—period.

"Okay—I go downstairs last night to get a sandwich," Art said, "and there they are in the family room with blueprints."

"What's a blueprint?"

"This big thing an architect draws—like for a new house."

"Are we getting a new house?" Lily said. "I like this one!"

"Don't get excited. From what I could gather, they're planning an addition to this house."

"Oh," Lily said. "That would be okay, I guess."

"Yeah, but the question is, why? I'm gonna be going off to college. You and Joe both have your own rooms already. How much house do they need?"

Lily cocked her head at him. "So what are you thinking?"

"I don't know," Art said. "But I think there's something brewing—something big. Just keep your eyes and ears open, okay?" He got up to go and then stopped. "And don't mention it to Joe. He's got a mouth like the Grand Canyon."

Lily nodded soberly, but she wasn't really thinking about Joe. As Art went for the door, she said, "Hey, Art, could I ask you something?"

76

"Who else would you ask? I'm only the smartest person in the house." Art held up a hand, "Okay, besides Dad. That's not fair, though—he's got a Ph.D."

"Did anybody ever say you were weird?" Lily said.

Art let out a guffaw. "You gotta be kidding. Not lately."

"Yeah, but what about like when you were in middle school? Did people say you were weird because you walked around with a saxophone case?"

Art nodded. "Yeah, but then I turned 'weird' into an art form and everybody wanted to do it."

Lily sighed.

"Somebody's calling you a weirdo, I take it," Art said.

"Yeah."

"So go with it. If you're weird, flaunt it."

"How do I do that?" Lily said.

Art sat back down on the bed. "Why are they saying you're weird?"

"Because I had an idea about our scene for Shakespeare. Stuff like that."

"Oh—so you're a weird actor type. That's easy. Just start dressing like a weird actor. When somebody says something to you about you being a wacko, just throw a couple of your Shakespeare lines in their face. They'll give it up after a while—or else start doing it too." Art leaned lazily against the bedpost. "It's all about attitude and confidence. If you let them beat you down, you haven't got a chance."

Lily thought about that for a long time after Art left, even after she'd written a prayer in her journal and turned out the light.

It made sense, really. Reni didn't seem to care if people thought she was a violin freak. Art definitely didn't mind if people called him a band geek.

The problem was, Lily didn't know what a weird actor type looked like. She didn't even know where to start putting together an outfit an actress would wear to school.

"I gotta do some research," Lily whispered to Otto.

She listened. The whole house was quiet, and she'd heard Mom and Dad go into their room a half hour ago. Silently, she slipped out of bed and fumbled in the dark for a pad and pencil. With Otto right behind her, she crept down the stairs to the family room. David Letterman was just coming on TV and introducing a new teen actress.

Lily had to fight to keep her eyes open, but she sat up straight and took notes.

The actress's hair was flying all over the place. That shouldn't be too hard. Lily just wouldn't wear any clips to try to tame hers. She also looked like she'd used a lot of imagination when she'd picked out her clothes. She had on boots up to her thighs and a vest that was almost as long as her very short skirt. The colors were bright and didn't necessarily match—but in a way they went together.

Lily was trying to get all of that down when Otto perked up his ears and growled. Lily snapped off the remote and held her breath. Mom and Dad weren't going to be thrilled to find her up this late.

Otto growled again, and this time, Lily heard a noise—coming from outside.

Is that stupid dog across the street getting into our garbage again? Lily thought.

She tiptoed to the window, Otto still growling at her heels, and bent one of the slats in the blinds so she could look out. She was just in time to see something long and white fly by.

Lily jumped back, and Otto scrambled to get under the coffee table. Lily's heart started to pound. What was *that*?

She peered out between the slats again, and once more a white thing sailed past. It was a roll of toilet paper.

Lily yanked the blinds up and stared out in disbelief. The whole front yard was a sea of Charmin, with pieces blowing from branches in the wind and half-rolled-out rolls littering the ground. She could hear laughter and footsteps fading into the night.

Lily ran to the front door and fumbled with the locks to get it open. She started to step out onto the front porch, but she nearly fell over something parked right in the way. Lily put her hand over her mouth to keep from screaming. She was looking down into an old toilet.

Lily started to turn and run back into the house — back to where she was before she knew someone had tee-peed her house — the biggest insult a middle-schooler could suffer. But even as she turned, she spotted a piece of paper inside the toilet.

Using only the tips of her fingers, Lily plucked it out and unfolded it. THIS IS WHERE YOUR ACTING BELONGS, the note said in bold black letters. It was signed, THE SHAKESPEER CLUB.

Lily sank down onto the concrete porch and pulled her knees up under her chin, shivering in the cold.

They really do hate me, she thought as the tears came. *They think I'm so weird that they want me out of the club.*

Inside the house, Otto was barking to get out and join her, but Lily couldn't get up to shut him up. All she could do was rock back and forth and cry.

It wasn't long before the door opened and Mom came out, hugging her bathrobe around her.

"Lily, what in the world?" she said. "What are you — "

She didn't have to finish. The toilet paper blowing in the November wind seemed to be explanation enough.

"Come inside, hon," Mom said. "Come on — we'll have some hot chocolate."

Lily got up and followed her. She was hiccupping from crying.

When they got to the kitchen and Mom put her head in the closet to look for the hot chocolate mix, she said, "Don't just assume this is about you, Lil. There are five of us living here, you know."

"It was for me," Lily said. "They left a note."

Mom pulled her head out of the closet and looked at the paper Lily flattened out on the table.

"Wow," Mom said. "They fight dirty, don't they?"

She put a cup of hot water into the microwave and sat down across from Lily.

"What's the fight about?" she said.

"They didn't like my idea for the theme!" Lily said. "But nobody else had any ideas!" She put head down on her arms. "They just think I'm weird."

"I'm really sorry this happened," Mom said.

Lily raised her head. "I know I'm not supposed to hate, Mom," she said tearfully. "But it's so hard not to sometimes."

"Oh, I know," Mom said. "I have the urge to hate now and then myself."

"What do you do?" Lily said.

"Well—after I storm around and slam cabinet doors and make everybody's life miserable," Mom said, mouth twitching, "I usually pray for whoever it is I want to hate."

"Wow," Lily said. "You're better than me."

"No—I've just had more practice."

"Are you sure that's the only way? Isn't there something else I can do?"

"If you want to do it the way Jesus told us to," Mom said, "then that's your answer." She cocked an eyebrow. "I assume you want to do it the Jesus way."

"Oh, yeah!" Lily said. "It's just gonna be hard."

"He never said it was going to be easy," Mom said.

The microwave beeped just then, and Mom got up to pour the mix in the hot water. Lily closed her eyes.

Okay, God, she prayed. *I don't really want to do this—but could you please help the people in the Shakespeare Club that hate my guts so much they'd tee-pee my yard and leave a toilet on my front porch?*

Mom set a cup of hot chocolate in front of Lily and looked again at the note.

"Huh," she said. "You'd think they could at least spell Shakespeare right."

Lily snatched up the note. S-H-A-K-E-S-P-E-E-R, it said. It was supposed to be P-E-A-R-E. Mrs. Reinhold had made sure everybody knew that, even Shad—

And then it hit her.

It wasn't the Shakespeare Club. It was probably Ashley and her group.

Ugh, Lily thought. *Does this mean I have to pray for them too?*

When she went back to bed, she did—but it was the hardest prayer she had ever prayed.

Lily woke up late the next morning, so she was the last one to the bench before school. Even Reni was there. Her orchestra teacher was absent so she couldn't practice in the music room, she said.

"What's the matter, Lily?" Suzy said, touching Lily on the arm.

Lily told them, and they listened with their mouths hanging open. When she was finished, Reni was the first one to speak.

"Girlz," she said, "this means war!"

"It does?" Suzy said. She was already looking as if she'd rather be at the dentist.

"Ya!" Kresha said.

Lily stared at Reni. "I thought you didn't think this was important enough for me to need protection," she said.

"I have *so* changed my mind!" Reni said. "This isn't just some little chicken note. They left a *toilet*, for Pete's sake."

"Ya!" Kresha said.

"Yeah," Zooey said, "but what are we going to do—toilet-paper Ashley's yard?"

81

Suzy let out a whimper.

"No," Reni said. "We don't lower ourselves — that's what my dad always says. We don't attack them — we just protect Lily — I mean, *really* protect her."

"But how?" Zooey said.

Reni pressed the dimples into her face as she thought. Lily wanted to hug her. It was just a little less painful now that Reni was really on her side again.

"Okay," Reni said finally. "Somebody has to be with Lily all the time. There's only two classes that one of us isn't in with her — music and study hall."

"I have first period on the same wing, though," Zooey said. "I could at least protect her in the hall." She stuck out her chest. "I'll get right between her and anybody that says a bad word to her."

If Lily hadn't been so grateful, she'd have laughed. She pretty much knew that Zooey would run at the first glimmer of a bad word — but it was the thought that counted.

The warning bell rang just then, and they scurried to gather up their backpacks.

"We'll work out the rest of the details at Girlz Only this afternoon," Reni said. "Be thinking about it — and everybody stay close to Lily."

"Wait," Lily said. "There's one more thing."

"Hurry, Lily," Suzy said. "We'll be late."

"We have to keep praying for Ashley and all of them."

"Gross me out!" Reni said.

"I know," Lily said, "but we have to."

Suzy nodded and began to edge away.

"One more thing," Lily said.

"Li-lee!"

Lily grinned at them. "Thanks, guys," she said.

And as she walked off to first period with Zooey stuck to her like Velcro, she silently thanked God too.

Chapter 11

Lily couldn't help being excited about the blocking rehearsal at lunch that day, and she hurried to get to Mrs. Reinhold's room the minute the bell rang. But somebody else had hurried even faster. Ashley and Shad were standing in the hall.

Lily whipped past them and tried not to look as she slipped into the room and shut the door behind her. But she couldn't resist one peek through the window in the door, just to make sure Ashley wasn't dragging Shad off by the ear or something.

She was relieved to see Shad still standing there, hands in his pockets, while Ashley flailed her arms and squawked in his face. Lily couldn't hear what she was saying, but whatever it was, it wasn't having much of an effect on Shad. He actually looked pretty bored.

Until Ashley stomped her foot.

Yikes, Lily thought, *I haven't seen anybody do that since Joe was four.*

It definitely got Shad's attention. He put his hand up—which in middle school sign language usually meant, "Get away from me with your garbage," and turned toward the door. Lily ducked.

"What are you doing?" somebody behind her said.

It was Natalie, scooting her glasses further up on her nose and looking through them at Lily as if she were examining a pimple in the mirror.

"Nothing," Lily said.

Natalie shifted her gaze to the window. "You were spying on Shad and his girlfriend."

Lily slunk away from the door just as it opened and the rest of the kids filed in. Shad trailed them as the bell rang, and just before the door shut, Lily heard Ashley say, "I am so not kidding, Shad!"

Ed slipped into a seat behind Shad. "Trouble with your chick, Petruchio?" he murmured.

"She ain't my chick no more," Shad said out of the side of his mouth.

Lily tried to focus on Mrs. Reinhold and her announcements, but her mind stuck stubbornly on Shad. They'd broken up? Just now—out in the hall? She didn't know anything about breakups, but maybe foot-stomping went along with them. The real question was, if Ashley and Shad had broken up, was that a good thing or a bad thing?

When Mrs. Reinhold finally finished talking—about what, Lily had no idea—she sent Hilary and Wesley into the hall with their coaches to work on their lines and the "old men" group and their coaches into another teacher's empty room. Ed, Victoria, Lily, and Shad had the "studio" all to themselves. Once they started working, Lily forgot all about Ashley.

Ed and Victoria explained each section of the blocking and demonstrated it, and then let Lily and Shad try it. It was the most fun Lily remembered having—well, maybe ever.

In the beginning, Lily—Kate—stood in the center, arms folded, face scowling as Shad—Petruchio—moved back and forth behind her, purring his flattering lines, until on her line, "Moved!" she threw back a hand, landing a stage punch right on Petruchio's jaw. Ed taught Shad how to do a pratfall back onto the couch. Even Lily had to admit he was good at it.

From there the back-and-forth chase was on as they vaulted over "couches" and held each other at bay with chairs.

It was all funny and pretty easy too, since Lily's natural instincts were usually to either run from Shad or clobber him anyway.

But, then, as they neared the end, Ed said to Shad, "All right, when you get to the line, 'Your father hath consented that you shall be my wife,' you back her onto the couch from the end here and get her pinned down."

"Whadda you mean, pinned down?" Shad said.

Yeah, Lily thought. She was starting to get nervous.

"Like a big St. Bernard would pin somebody down if he were going to lick their face," Ed said.

"I gotta lick her face?" Shad said.

Victoria laughed. "No—but that's the idea."

"Watch," Ed said.

He walked toward Victoria, and she backed away from him until she "tripped" over the end of the line-of-chairs couch and fell onto it. Ed kept moving toward her as she scooted backward toward the other end. He did look like an overgrown puppy ready to slobber on her cheeks.

"No way!" Lily said.

"Naw—that'll be cool!" Shad said, grinning.

Lily stared in surprise. Shad wasn't even pretending to lose his lunch.

"Try it," Victoria said. He winked at Lily. "And then I'll show you what you get to do."

Lily and Shad positioned themselves, and Shad immediately got into backing her toward the "couch." Lily managed the backward fall just the way Ed coached her and was more than willing to scoot backward with Shad charging toward her on all fours. It didn't seem to bother him that he was almost touching her, so Lily decided to go with it.

"Great!" Ed said. "I love it!"

"Okay—now—Kate!" Victoria said. Her voice was full of giggles. "When Petruchio says 'For I am born to tame you, Kate,' you get your foot up there, plant it right in the middle of his chest, and give him a shove!"

"Only don't really shove," Ed said. "Petruchio, it's your job to make it *look* like she's shoving you. It's all an illusion—and that way nobody gets hurt."

Bummer, Lily thought. But then the thought danced away. This really wasn't so bad. It was actually fun.

"Try it from 'Your father hath consented,'" Victoria said.

They scrambled off the couch, got ready, and did the moves, Shad rattling off his lines and backing her down, Lily reacting with scooting and an angry face. At just the right moment, she planted a foot on his chest, gave a gentle push, and Shad tumbled backwards, feet kicking in the air as he shouted out his lines. Ed and Victoria were doubled over and howling.

Shad, of course, got up and took several bows. Lily hung her head off the chair and giggled right from her belly.

That is, until her eyes fell on the window in the door. There was Ashley—eyes in slits so narrow Lily could barely see them. Her mouth was drawn up into a tight little knot and so was the fist she raised when she saw Lily looking at her. It froze the giggles right in Lily's throat.

Then Ashley disappeared from the window and the door flew open, letting in the rest of the actors and their coaches.

"Awesome work, you two," Ed said to Lily and Shad.

"Yeah, well, when you got it, you got it," Shad said.

He high-fived Ed and Victoria and even Lily, and went on to attempt to high-five Mrs. Reinhold. Lily could only mutter a weak "thanks." There was something about Ashley's face—and fist—that made Lily very sure she was more than talk or a toilet and a tee-peed yard. Lily might need the Girlz' protection after all.

"All right, people," Mrs. Reinhold was saying as they put the room back in order, "don't forget that we are going to need a props manager and a costume manager."

"What's she talking about?" Lily said.

She meant the question for Victoria, but Fiona turned to her, lip hanging in disgust.

"Weren't you listening at the beginning of the period?" she said.

She shook her head at Natalie, who said, "She wants the names of people who might wanna help us — but they have to be mature."

"It'll probably be eighth graders, though," Fiona said. "So don't worry about it."

"Oh," Lily said. "Okay."

The look Fiona and Natalie gave each other as they turned away stung, but Lily pushed that away. She had enough other things to worry about.

The bell rang and everybody crowded to the door, Lily among them. It was so much fun working on the scene, but once she was back with the whole group, she always felt like a sixth finger trying to fit into a five-fingered glove.

What if I had taken Art's advice and dressed like a funky actor? she thought. *They'd probably stuff me in the trash can.*

She got out of the room as quickly as she could and was headed through the crowd down the hall when she felt something hit her in the ankle. She pitched forward into the throng of students that clogged the hall, backpack dragging her one way and the traffic pulling her the other. She slid down the back of some girl's leg and hit the floor hands first. The minute her palms slapped the ground, someone's heel came down on her left thumb.

"Hey, klutz!" somebody yelled.

There was only laughter until a pair of hands pulled her up by her right arm and guided her out of the tangle of students. It was Ed, with Victoria right beside him.

"You all right?" Ed said.

Although she wasn't quite sure, Lily nodded. This had to be the most embarrassing thing in life, and the sooner people—especially *these* people—stopped looking at her, the sooner she could crawl into the nearest litter bin and die.

"A person could get killed out here," Ed said.

Victoria put her arm around Lily's shoulder and straightened her backpack. "What happened?" she said.

"I tripped over something," Lily said. "I'm the biggest spastic."

"No, you are *not*," Victoria said.

Lily looked at her in surprise.

"You aren't even a little bit spastic," Victoria said. "You picked up on the blocking and everything so fast today—you're really coordinated."

"I am?" Lily said. Wait 'til she informed Joe of *that*.

Victoria put her hand on Lily's arm. "Did somebody trip you, Lily?" she said.

Lily felt her eyes widening. "I don't think so."

"You mean on purpose?" Ed said.

"You've seen the way these kids treat each other," Victoria said. She flipped her braid over her shoulder. "I wouldn't put it past somebody to try to take her down."

Ed grinned. "What did you do, Lily, steal some girl's boyfriend?"

Lily put her hand over her mouth so they wouldn't see it dropping open.

"You're embarrassing her, Ed!" Victoria said. She put her hands on Lily's shoulders. "Hang in there, Lily. Middle school won't last forever."

"Okay," Lily said. "I really do hafta go—"

"Go!" Ed said. "And watch your step!"

Lily heard Victoria smack him as she hurried off toward math class. But what stayed in her ears were Victoria's words: *Did somebody trip you, Lily?*

Did somebody? Somebody like — Ashley?

Ashley had been lurking around. She'd seen enough of Lily and Shad's scene to want to make a scene of her own.

Lily stopped dead in front of the math room.

Shad said they'd broken up — but what if that wasn't a good thing? What if Ashley blamed that on Lily?

A hand reached out the door and grabbed Lily's arm, pulling her inside just as the bell rang. Reni was searching Lily's face with her eyes.

"Where have you been?" she said.

Lily looked at her. Her face felt like a piece of wood.

"I think I'm in trouble," she said. "Big trouble."

Chapter 12

From that moment on, the Girlz didn't leave Lily alone for a second, except when she was in her own house—and even then Kresha was constantly looking over her shoulder as if Ashley were going to pop out of Lily's closet. It took a while for Lily to get her to concentrate on the scene.

"We have to practice moving around while we're saying the lines," Lily said.

"I can learn," Kresha said.

Lily shoved all her stuff against the walls in her room and designated the bed as the couch and China, her huge stuffed panda, as a second chair since she had only the one actual chair from her desk. It was more cramped than the studio, but that wasn't their biggest problem. They got halfway into the scene, and Lily couldn't remember what move came next.

"I should've written it down," she said. "I just thought I'd remember."

Kresha pointed to her forehead and frowned. "Think, Lily."

"I'm trying. I could call Shad—"

She looked at Kresha.

"Nah," they both said.

"I've got an idea, though," Lily said. "I'll ask Mrs. Reinhold if you can watch my rehearsal tomorrow."

"I can protect you there!" Kresha said.

"I don't think Ashley's gonna try anything there."

But Kresha's frown grew deeper, until she looked almost as grim as Deputy Dog. "We be careful," she said. "Ashley is evil."

Lily and Kresha announced their plan to Suzy and Zooey the next morning at the bench. The minute they did, Lily saw Suzy and Zooey shrink down like a pair of beach balls with the air going out of them.

Uh-oh, Lily thought. *Now they really feel left out.*

"I wish we could watch too," Zooey said.

"You can guard the door outside," Kresha said.

Neither of them looked too enthusiastic about that, especially Suzy. What was she going to do up against Ashley anyway? Zooey might try to distract her with her latest outfit, but Suzy—

Suddenly, Lily stopped. "Hey," she said. "You guys wanna help with the play?"

"No," Suzy said. "I'd be so scared!"

"Not act," Lily said. "Be the prop manager. And Zooey, you could be the costume manager. Mrs. Reinhold told us to try to get people."

"What would I have to prop up?" Suzy said.

Lily could feel herself straightening importantly. "Props are the things we use in the play, like the pillow I throw at Shad, that kind of stuff."

"Oh," Suzy said. She looked a little less terrified.

"I would get to take care of the costumes?" Zooey said. Her face was already glowing with what Lily knew were visions of satin dresses and velvet capes. Why hadn't she thought of this before? Zooey was perfect.

"Everybody's supposed to suggest people, and Mrs. Reinhold picks," Lily said, "but if you come to rehearsal and she sees you, you know, maybe she'll pick you guys."

Zooey was already bouncing like she had springs on her fashionable ankle-high boots, and even Suzy looked kind of excited.

"She will choose them!" Kresha said. "I know!"

"Yeah, well, we better be praying," Lily said. "And don't forget — we gotta be praying for Ashley and all them too."

Kresha scowled. "Too hard."

"That's for sure," Zooey said.

"Well, Girlz," Lily said, straightening up again. "Jesus didn't say it would be easy."

"Preaching a sermon, Robbins?" somebody said.

"No," Lily said, closing her eyes. Ugh. It was Chelsea.

"Sure sounded like it. Isn't that against the law or something?"

Lily opened her eyes to answer her. There was Kresha right in front of her, her back to Lily. Suzy and Zooey were on either side, their shoulders touching Lily's. Suzy was staring at the floor as if she wished it would open up and swallow her, but she was there.

"Leave Lily alone," Kresha said.

"Yeah," Zooey said.

"Who's gonna make me?" Chelsea said.

"We are," Kresha said.

"This little pack of weirdos? I don't *think* so!" Lily saw Chelsea flick her hand as if she were dismissing a swarm of flies. "She's a wuss," she said, flicking at Suzy and then turning to Zooey. "She walks around in clothes that are *way* too good for her — and *you* can barely even talk right. Give it up!"

With a click of her tongue, Chelsea moved off. Kresha started after her, but all three of the Girlz grabbed at different parts of her jacket and held her back.

"I want to go!" Kresha said. "I want to — pull off her nose!"

"No, Kresha!" Suzy said. "Reni said we can't lower ourselves."

Lily nodded in agreement, although she had to admit she'd like to see Chelsea without a nose. Chelsea had cut Lily's friends down in the ways it would hurt them most. Being noseless actually sounded too good for Chelsea.

"You know what, Lily?" Zooey said, looking down at her new Limited Too skirt and her even newer Old Navy sweater.

"What?" Lily said.

"It's gonna be really hard to pray for somebody I hate so much."

Lily had to agree to that too.

But she did pray that Mrs. Reinhold would pick Zooey and Suzy, and that she'd let Kresha watch rehearsals. That was easy—and it kept her from wishing various features on Chelsea's face would fall off.

Even Reni accompanied the Girlz to Mrs. Reinhold's room at lunch just to be sure nobody would try to take Lily out at the ankles again. There was no sign of Ashley or any of her friends, though, and Reni told them before she rushed off to the orchestra room that that was a good sign. Lily sure hoped so.

The other good sign was that nobody else in the Shakespeare group appeared to have brought in possible prop and costume managers. Just to be on the safe side, Lily dragged Zooey and Suzy up to Mrs. Reinhold right away.

"I brought people, like you said, Mrs. Reinhold," Lily said. "Zooey could do costumes and Suzy could do props. I told her what they were."

"I'm sure you did," Mrs. Reinhold said. "Why don't you girls have a seat and we'll see what everyone else has come up with."

"They're really hard workers," Lily said as Suzy and Zooey hurried to the back of the room. "And I know they're responsible."

"If they're friends of yours, Lilianna," Mrs. Reinhold said, "I'm sure they are."

Lily nodded and went to her seat beside Victoria.

"She's such a kiss-up," she heard Natalie whisper.

"Just what we need," Fiona whispered back, "two of her weird little friends."

Don't they care that I can totally hear them? Lily thought. *I just hate—*

There was that "h" word again. Lily sighed. The list of people she had to pray for was getting longer by the minute.

The bell rang, and Shad sat up on the back of the desk chair. "We gotta start rehearsin', Mrs. R," he said.

"*Gotta*, Mr. Shifferdecker?" she said, motioning for him to sit down.

"Okay—hafta."

Mrs. Reinhold peered at him through her glasses. "I suppose that's an improvement."

"We're working on it," Ed said. Then he and Shad high-fived each other.

"Male bonding," Victoria whispered to Lily.

"We have some housekeeping details to deal with first," Mrs. Reinhold said. "I trust you have all brought me the names of potential prop and costume managers."

She surveyed the class, and Lily looked around too. Only Gary was raising his hand. Lily glanced nervously at Zooey and Suzy, who were clutching each other's arms.

"Yes?" Mrs. Reinhold said, nodding at Gary.

"Ashley Adamson and Chelsea—I forget her last name," Gary said.

Lily stopped breathing. She didn't dare look back at the Girlz now. Suzy had probably crawled inside the desk at the mere mention of their names. Lily clutched the top of her desk until her knuckles went white.

"You are acquainted with these ladies?" Mrs. Reinhold said to Gary.

Gary shook his shaved head. "Not exactly," he said. "They just came up to me in the hall and said they wanted to do it. They said they heard you wanted people."

"How can you recommend them if you don't know them?" Mrs. Reinhold said.

Gary grinned. "They're babes."

Hilary slapped him on the arm.

Oh, Lily thought. *Hilary and Gary must be going out.*

"I'm not sure that is the criterion we are using," Mrs. Reinhold said in a dry voice.

"You don't want them two chicks anyway," Shad said.

"*Those* two chicks," Ed muttered to him.

"You don't think they'll work well for us, Mr. Shifferdecker?" Mrs. Reinhold said.

Shad looked at her as if she'd suggested a chess tournament.

"No," he said.

"I'm inclined to agree," she said. "Any other nominations?"

Lily raised her hand. She was sure she heard some muffled groans.

"Oh, yes," Mrs. Reinhold said. "Lilianna has brought in the ladies in the back—Suzy Wheeler and Zooey—"

"Hoffman," Lily said.

"They come highly recommended by Lilianna," Mrs. Reinhold said.

"They're seventh graders," Natalie said.

"Yes?" Mrs. Reinhold said.

"Well—that's the point." Natalie looked around, and several people nodded.

"I don't see that as a problem," Mrs. Reinhold said. "Shad and Lilianna are seventh graders, and so far they have outshone everyone. That would make their grade level a positive as I see it." She looked around, eyebrows raised. "Any other nominees?"

Fiona raised her hand. Lily tightened her grip on the desk.

"I have a couple of friends who'd be really good," Fiona said. "I could probably talk them into it."

"I'm not certain we want someone who has to be talked into it," Mrs. Reinhold said, "particularly when we already have two people who look eager to assist us."

Lily glanced back. Suzy and Zooey were on the edges of their seats, and Zooey was nodding like a dashboard dog with a spring in its neck.

"Nobody's 'eager' to work on Shakespeare unless you talk 'em into it like you did us," Wesley said.

"Did you have to talk your friends into coming, Lilianna?" Mrs. Reinhold said.

"No," Lily said. "They wanted to."

"Figures," she heard Natalie mutter.

Mrs. Reinhold looked sharply at Natalie and then gave a brisk nod.

"I think we have our prop and costume managers," she said. "Suzy, Zooey, the three of us will chat while everyone rehearses. We have a great deal of work to do."

Lily swiveled around in her desk, as much to avoid the eighth graders' rolling eyes as to see Zooey and Suzy's sparkling ones.

"Mrs. Reinhold," Natalie said.

"I've made my decision," Mrs. Reinhold said.

"No — it's not about that. Who is she?"

Lily turned to see Natalie pointing to Kresha, who was still sitting by the door. Lily had forgotten all about her.

"That's my friend, Kresha," Lily said. "She helps me run lines, and I wanted her to see our blocking so we can practice at home. Is that okay?"

"It's lovely," Mrs. Reinhold said. "You are more than welcome, Kresha."

"So — can we bring in friends too?" Philip said.

"Do you have friends who are helping you at home with your scene?" Mrs. Reinhold asked.

Philip gave her an embarrassed grin. "I haven't even told my friends I'm doing this. They'll think I'm a geek."

"Then why did you even ask?" Mrs. Reinhold said.

"Are we supposed to be practicing at home?" Fiona said.

"It certainly wouldn't hurt you," Mrs. Reinhold said. "It seems to be helping Shad and Lilianna."

Wesley laughed out loud. "Like Shifferdecker practices Shakespeare at home!"

"Not at *his* home," Ed said. "Mine."

He and Shad high-fived each other. The whole room fell into a stunned silence.

"All right, people," Mrs. Reinhold said. "We have a little more than a week. Let's get to work."

That "little more than a week" soared by the way days do when everything is going well.

Suzy was organized and efficient with the props. Carrying around a clipboard gave her a certain look of power.

Zooey busily added touches of lace and trim to the costumes Mrs. Reinhold brought in and helped everybody get fitted. Lily didn't say it out loud, but she thought her costume was the best one. It was hot pink with a lace-up vest built right into it. Leaping over the couch wearing it made the scene that much more hilarious, and even Mrs. Reinhold burst out laughing when she saw it. *That* wasn't something you heard too often.

Mrs. Reinhold worked with two of her other eighth graders on the time capsule scenes, and the whole group met after school in the wood shop to help build and paint the capsule itself. Lily said it was completely cool the way the top opened so they could climb out, which got Natalie and Fiona's eyes nearly rolling out onto the floor.

"This is like something they'd do in fifth grade," Lily heard Natalie tell Fiona.

"Yeah, well, doesn't it figure?" Fiona said.

No, it does not 'figure'! Lily wanted to yell at her.

But she soothed the hurt of that kind of comment by reassuring herself that she was going to show them all on Festival Day, especially when Mrs. Reinhold described the possible prizes they could win.

"There will be an award for best overall presentation," she said. "One for most creative theme—"

"We won't be getting *that* one," Natalie muttered.

"Then there will be individual awards for actors."

Lily closed her eyes. She could see herself in her long Shakespearean dress, humbly accepting the award for best actress and refusing to look smug, as Natalie and Fiona and the rest of them watched in envy.

Lily called that image up a lot during that week, especially when Fiona and Natalie got to rolling their eyes. She tried to remember to pray for them, but like she told Otto on several occasions when she was writing prayers in her journal, "Zooey was right: it's so hard to pray for people you hate. Okay—not hate—can't stand."

Still, the preparations were mostly fun. It was pretty impossible for Ashley or her friends to do anything to Lily with the Girlz guarding her like Secret Service agents. There were plenty of evil looks from Ashley and Chelsea, but even the day the school pictures came back, Lily controlled her temper.

Mrs. Reinhold handed them out during third period. The second she turned her back after putting Lily's envelope on her desk, Ashley turned around and snatched it up, before Lily had a chance to get a glimpse of it herself. Ashley let out a laugh that spattered little droplets of spit all over the front of the packet.

"Give it back, Ashley," Lily said through her teeth.

She made a grab for the envelope, but Ashley held it out of her reach.

"Get a grip," Ashley said. "You look like you're about to attack somebody!"

I am gonna attack somebody if you don't hand it over! Lily thought. But she sat back in her desk and folded her arms. If she got into it with

Ashley right here in Mrs. Reinhold's classroom, she was going to get in trouble—and that meant no Shakespeare.

You'd like that, wouldn't you, Ashley? Lily thought. *Well, no way!*

Ashley was still studying Lily's face, which glared out from the opening in the envelope, and she was still laughing uncontrollably. Lily could clearly see it now, and it was definitely the worst school picture yet—even worse than first grade when she'd had no front teeth. In this one, her eyes were narrowed into beady-blue points, and her mouth was drawn so tightly it made little pucker lines under her nose.

Is that what I look like when I'm hating somebody? she thought. *Gross me out and make me icky!*

She put her hand up to her mouth. Did she look like that right now? Probably so—since she was shooting eye-bullets into the side of Ashley's head.

Yikes, she thought. *Hate looks ugly.*

Lily immediately fixed a smile on her face. "Could I have those back now, please?" she said.

"Uh, yeah," Ashley said, tossing them onto Lily's desk. "I sure don't want them!"

Lily turned the envelope over so she couldn't see her pruned-up face. *I sure don't either,* she thought.

Mrs. Reinhold handed Ashley her pictures just then, and Ashley turned her back on Lily, shielding her envelope with her hand.

I'm not going to lower myself, Lily thought.

Besides—if making fun of Lily's pictures was the worst Ashley could come up with, what was there to worry about? She'd obviously gotten the message from the way the Girlz were protecting her and Lily's refusal to take her bait.

At least Lily thought so—until the Wednesday before the festival—when Ashley showed her there was a great deal to worry about.

Chapter 13

On Wednesday morning, Lily woke up with the cold Joe had brought home and generously passed through the family. She was blowing her nose in the bathroom when Mom pushed the door open a crack and poked in a bottle of Day-Quil and a glass of orange juice.

"You probably ought to stay home," she said. "Everybody else was in bed for at least a day."

"Not me!" Lily said. "I can't miss any rehearsals."

"I'm sure Mrs. Reinhold would make an exception if you're sick."

"I'm not sick—I just have a cold," Lily said. "I'm not a wimp like Joe and Art."

"Do you want me to pass that information along to them?"

Lily could imagine Mom's mouth twitching on the other side of the door.

Lily loaded up with Kleenex and cough drops and took off for school. Kresha, as always, was waiting at the bench to go over lines. The more they did it, the more the words sang in Lily's head like a song she was sure she'd never forget. Even Kresha could do it without the script. It was like a duet they knew by heart.

Right after Suzy and Zooey arrived — Suzy with her clipboard and Zooey with the pile of dry-cleaning bags she'd brought to protect everybody's costumes on the way to the festival on Saturday — Deputy Dog made her usual stop.

"You two are getting better at this every day," she said when Lily and Kresha had finished their line run. "You're a couple of pros."

"What is *pro?*" Kresha said.

Deputy Dog never had a chance to answer. Suddenly there was a ruckus on the stairs. Ashley Adamson's voice shrieked over all the other before-school noise.

"Sha-ad!" she said. "Let go — we'll get in trouble!"

Lily gasped, right out loud. Shad and Ashley's fingers were tightly entwined as they both came down the steps. Shad's face was dark red, almost purple, and Ashley had both hands around his as he plunged on, as if she were using one to try to pry the other loose from Shad's grip.

For a crazy moment, Lily looked at Deputy Dog, on the ridiculous chance that she didn't see them. But the officer was staring right at them, and her thumbs had already gone to her belt. *Not* a good sign.

Let go of her, Shad! Lily wanted to scream. *You can't get in trouble!*

But not only did Shad not let go — he stopped at the bottom of the steps and grabbed Ashley by the wrist with his other hand. It was a confusing tangle of palms and fingers. It couldn't have been a better example of physical contact if they'd been wrestling on the ground.

Deputy Dog was on them in a slick minute. Lily watched in horror as she snatched Shad by the back of his T-shirt and said, "Turn loose, Shifferdecker!"

Shad gave his arm a wrench and then grabbed onto his own hand as if it had been caught in a car door. Ashley mercly pulled hers behind her back and smiled at Deputy Dog.

Smiled.

"Look at her!" Zooey whispered to Lily. "She's practically laughing!"

It did appear that Ashley was having the time of her life as Deputy Dog put a hand against her back and a hand around Shad's arm and led them both in the direction of the office. Even as Lily and the Girlz stared after her, Ashley flipped a glance over her shoulder at them and grinned.

"Evil!" Kresha said.

"I don't get it," Zooey said. "She's about to get suspended for physical contact, and she looks all happy!"

"I'd be dying," Suzy said.

Lily sank down onto the bench and put her face in her hands, head pounding.

"What's wrong, Lily?" Zooey said. "Aren't you happy to see them get busted?"

"Ashley," Lily said. "Not Shad. If he gets suspended, we don't get to do our scene. We all signed a contract saying we wouldn't get in any trouble before the festival." She dug for a tissue and miserably blew her nose.

Zooey sat down and put her arm around her. "I'm sorry, Lily," she said.

Suzy sat on the other side. "Why would Shad do that? I thought you said they broke up."

Lily nodded. "They did. I haven't seen them together in about a week."

"He picked a fine time to get back together with her," Zooey said.

Kresha folded her arms against her chest and grunted. She was still standing up, staring at the stairs as if the Shad-Ashley scene were still going on.

"She hold *him!*" she said. "He pull—ugh—like this!"

"What's she talking about?" Zooey muttered.

"You're saying *she* was holding onto *him*, and *he* was trying to pull away?" Suzy said.

"Ya," Kresha said.

"But she was saying, 'Shad, let go!' " Zooey said.

"She lie," Kresha said.

Lily stared at her. "You mean, you think she set the whole thing up? Planned it that way?"

"How you say — pretend?" Kresha said.

"Oh." Zooey's eyes grew round. "But why would she get her own self in trouble?"

"Because she doesn't care what she has to do," Lily said, "as long as she keeps Shad from doing that scene with me."

"We tell Deputy Dog!" Kresha said.

She actually started to march toward the office, fists doubled, but Lily jumped up and grabbed her by the arm.

"That's not gonna do any good!" she said. "Ashley will just deny it."

"And Shad did grab her wrist," Suzy said.

"Probably to try to get away! And she knew Deputy Dog comes down here every day too." Zooey's eyes were rounder than ever. "You're right, Kresha — she *is* evil!"

They were convinced, but there was nothing they could do, and they were all miserable as they hauled themselves off to first period. The morning dragged in an agony of not knowing, but the agony of finding out for sure was even worse. At lunch, Mrs. Reinhold took Lily aside and told her Shad had been suspended.

"Does that mean we don't get to do our scene?" Lily said.

Mrs. Reinhold's face was long. "I'm afraid it does. I wish there was something I could do, Lilianna, after you've worked so hard." She brushed her hand against Lily's arm. "But I cannot make an exception. Shad signed a contract. I really thought he was going to make it."

She actually sounded sad, but Lily was sadder. She sagged into her desk and put her face in her hands.

"Suzy," she heard Mrs. Reinhold say, "take Lilianna to the restroom."

Suzy touched Lily's arm, but Lily put her face down on the desk, shielded herself with her arms, and quietly sobbed.

"I'll go get you some tissue," Suzy whispered, and disappeared.

Ed and Victoria both came by to try to talk to Lily, but she just shook her head. Kresha sat on one side of her, muttering in Croatian under her breath, and Zooey sat on the other side, rubbing Lily's back.

"Zooey — Kresha!" she heard Suzy hiss from the doorway.

They both got up and left, but Lily didn't. She was too disappointed to move.

A few minutes later, all three of them were back at her side. Kresha took Lily's head in her hands and lifted it up.

"Leave me alone!" Lily said angrily.

But Zooey shushed her, and Kresha shoved a wad of tissue into Lily's face.

"Listen to Suzy!" Zooey whispered.

Lily suddenly realized they were all on the edges of their seats as if they were sitting on springs.

"What?" Lily said.

Kresha nudged Suzy. "Tell!" she said.

Suzy's face was absolutely vanilla-colored, and she was clasping and unclasping her hands in her lap. She opened her mouth, but for a second nothing would come out, and Kresha gave her another impatient nudge.

"I was in the bathroom getting you some tissue," Suzy said finally. "And I heard Chelsea and Bernadette come in, so I closed the stall door."

Lily nodded.

"They were talking — and Chelsea was telling Bernadette how Ashley planned the whole thing so Shad would get in trouble."

"What else did they say?" Lily said.

"Just that Chelsea thought Ashley was, like, brilliant, because not only did she get back at Shad for breaking up with her, but she got back at you too."

Lily stopped crying and leaned back in her seat. "Kresha—you were right," she said.

Kresha grinned and raised her hand like a champion.

"But what good does it do?" Lily said. "I can't go to Deputy Dog and say somebody told me that she heard somebody else say that Ashley set it up."

Zooey and Kresha looked at Suzy.

"What?" Lily said.

Suzy looked down at her hands. "I'll tell her," she said.

Her voice was so timid, Lily could barely hear her. What she did hear she didn't believe.

"I can't ask you to do that, Suzy," Lily said. "I know you're scared of her."

"It's okay," she said. "You'd do it for me—any of you guys would. We're a team."

"We go with you," Kresha said.

But Suzy shook her head. "That'll make it look like we all made it up."

"You're gonna go by yourself?" Lily said.

Suzy couldn't even answer this time. She just nodded. But then she got up and went to Mrs. Reinhold's desk. "May I have a hall pass to the office?" she said.

The Girlz watched as Suzy took the pass and went, white-faced, out the door.

"We pray," Kresha said.

The three of them held hands and bowed their heads, and Lily whispered prayers. Behind her, she heard Natalie say, "Oh, brother!" but she didn't care.

Suzy didn't come back before the end of lunch, and in math class Lily nervously filled Reni in.

"*No*, she did *not* go to the office by herself!" Reni said.

"She *so* did."

Reni looked impressed for about a minute. Then she said, "It might not work, you know. If Ashley says Chelsea was lying, that could be the end of it."

Lily felt herself sagging. "You think so?"

"It could happen. Those girls aren't loyal to each other like we are."

Lily gave a sad nod.

Reni touched her hand. "Lil?" she said. "I'm sorry I was all conceited and snotty about this acting thing in the beginning. This really was important to you, huh?"

"Yeah," Lily said. She reached for a tissue again. "I guess it doesn't matter now, since it isn't gonna happen anyway."

"Matters to me," Reni said. "I don't want to be a stinky friend."

Sixth period, Suzy was there, and all the Girlz closed in on her the minute she walked in the door. She shook her head at all their questions until she got to her seat. She definitely looked like she needed to sit down.

"Hurry up and tell us!" Reni said. "Before the bell rings!"

"Don't anybody interrupt her," Zooey said.

"Okay," Suzy said. "They made me stay there while they called in Chelsea—and then Bernadette."

"Oh, no!" Zooey said. "Were you about to die?"

Kresha poked her, and Suzy went on.

"Chelsea said I was lying—but Bernadette told them the whole conversation almost exactly the way I told it."

Reni grabbed Lily's arm and squeezed it.

"Then they brought Ashley in."

"No!" all four of them said.

"They put me in another room. I could hear everything they were saying, but she didn't know I was there. They told her 'somebody' had snitched that she set the whole thing up. They told her *two* people had, but she still said she didn't."

They all wilted, but Suzy held up her hand. "I'm not done," she said.

The bell rang, and the Girlz all looked at each other with stricken faces. Reni waved her hand at Mr. Nutting.

"Could we just have five minutes to finish this conversation?" she said. "It's way important."

"If I say no, am I going to be looking at all of you passing notes to each other the entire period? Never mind—you have until I finish checking the roll."

"Talk fast," Reni said to Suzy.

Kresha put her hand over Zooey's mouth.

"Then they brought Shad in," Suzy said, "and said for him to tell what happened, since he hadn't said anything at all this morning, but he still wouldn't say anything—until Ashley started laughing."

"Laughing?" Zooey said between Kresha's fingers.

"I guess that made Shad mad, because he said she grabbed *him* and dragged *him* down the stairs and made it seem like *he* was dragging *her*, and he only grabbed her by the wrist to get away. He told it just like me and Bernadette both told it." Suzy took a big breath. It was the most Lily had ever heard her talk at one time. "Then they sent me back to class."

"So you don't know what happened yet?" Lily said.

Suzy shook her head. Evidently, she'd used up all her words.

"Time's up," Mr. Nutting said.

The Girlz reluctantly turned around in their seats and opened their science books. Lily stared at the page on the classification of animals, but all she could see was herself at the festival—one minute bowing on stage in her beautiful dress, the next sitting in the back of the theater crying, while the other kids did their scenes.

That afternoon after school, Lily skipped Girlz Club and, of course, rehearsing with Kresha, and went straight home. She took some more Day-Quil, although she didn't see how it was doing any good, and curled up in bed next to Otto and cried some more. She cried until her head ached and she fell asleep.

When she woke up, Mom had her hand on Lily's forehead.

"You're burning up," she said. "I think you're running a fever."

"No," Lily said "It's just 'cause I've been crying all day."

She told Mom the whole story, which only got her tearing up again. Mom got up and pulled some pajamas out of a drawer and handed them to her.

"You know what?" Lily said as she pulled off her sweater. "I don't think praying for your enemies works."

"It takes time," Mom said.

"But I don't have time! It's too late."

Mom sat on the edge of the bed and folded the clothes Lily was tossing as she took them off.

"You don't just pray for your enemies so things will be easier for *you*," Mom said. "I told you, Jesus never said it would be easy."

"Then I just don't get why we're supposed to do it," Lily said.

She pulled on her pajama top and grabbed a Kleenex to blow her nose. Otto cocked his head at her, and dove for the trash can when she dropped the tissue into it.

"Gross," Lily said.

Mom put the wastebasket up on Lily's desk. "We do it," she said, "because that's what Jesus did. That's the only way we'll know his kind of love."

Lily grunted.

"Do you still think you 'hate' Ashley and Chelsea after you've been praying for them?" Mom said.

"Yes!" Lily said.

"Then you need to pray more," Mom said. "It's really hard to hate somebody you're sincerely praying for."

Mom pulled the covers up to Lily's chin, kissed her on the forehead, and left to get some 7-Up and chicken noodle soup, the usual diet when somebody in the Robbins' house was sick.

Lily stared at the ceiling.

I might as well pray for them, she thought. *I don't have anything else to do now — except cry.*

And crying only made her head and chest hurt. She closed her eyes and tried — hard — to ask Jesus to do whatever it was he had to do to make Chelsea and Ashley act more like him.

"I'm asking for a miracle, I know," she prayed. "But they need it. They're always curling their lips and getting in trouble and wanting things like boyfriends that just seem like they make their lives a bunch of fighting and arguing — plus they aren't even loyal to each other — "

Lily stopped praying and opened her eyes.

Yikes, she thought, *it must really be a bummer to be them.*

Maybe she ought to be praying that God would make them happier. She was trying to hear what God might have to say about Chelsea and Ashley actually being happy when Mom came in carrying the phone. She was smiling.

"For you, Lil," she said.

"I don't feel like talking to anybody," Lily said.

"Oh — I think you'll want to talk to this lady," Mom said.

Lily took the phone and said hello.

"Lilianna?"

It was Mrs. Reinhold. Lily sat up straight in the bed.

"I've just gotten word from the office that Shad has been released from suspension. Apparently, he was framed — "

"So that means we get to do the scene in the festival?" Lily said.

"Yes, it does," Mrs. Reinhold said.

If Lily hadn't known better, she'd have thought Mrs. R was smiling.

"It sounds like you're as happy as I am," Mrs. Reinhold said.

109

"Do you just want to run up and down the hall and tell everybody?" Lily said.

"Not quite."

"Then I'm happier than you are," Lily said.

"You wonderful, obsessive child. Now get some rest. Take care of that cold."

When they hung up, Mom's mouth was doing its thing.

"What?" Lily said.

"I was imagining Mrs. Reinhold running up and down the hall shouting." Mom shook her head. "But if anybody could get her to do it, Lil, it would definitely be you."

Lily immediately wanted to call each of the Girlz and tell them, but Mom would only let her call Suzy and let her spread the word.

"You're not going to get over that cold running your mouth a hundred miles an hour. And if you're not better tomorrow, you are not going to school."

The good news alone made Lily feel better, and talking to Suzy made it even better than better.

"You were so brave," Lily told her. "If it weren't for you, I wouldn't be getting to do this."

"You know what, Lily?" Suzy said. "It really wasn't so bad. They were way nice to me. Deputy Dog sat right next to me, and if anybody started to look mean, it was like she was growling at them."

When they hung up, Lily prayed for Deputy Dog too.

Chapter

14

The next day at rehearsal, even the eighth graders were happy that Shad and Lily's scene was back in. They all high-fived Shad, however, and just sort of nodded at Lily. That was okay — she was too busy trying to keep from putting her head down on the desk.

She'd managed to convince Mom to let her go to school, promising to call her if she felt worse. But every chance she got she rested, and Mrs. Reinhold even let her suck on cough drops during class. There was no Ashley there to call her "teacher's pet." Then at lunch Lily put on her costume just like everyone else and let Zooey lace up the bodice.

"You're gonna have to wear makeup on Saturday," Zooey said. "Your nose is bright red."

"She's *supposed* to be ugly," Shad said.

Lily started to give him her Shad look, but the expression that suddenly came over his face stopped her. He looked just a little bit sorry.

"I don't think I heard you right, Pal," Ed said.

"You don't look all *that* ugly," Shad said to Lily.

"Thanks," Lily said.

After all, for Shad Shifferdecker, that was pretty good.

The dress rehearsal went well, and even the other scenes were polished and fun. During hers, Lily had to stop once to cough, and she was breathing hard when they were finished. Still, when they gave comments on each other's scenes at the end, Lily raised her hand a lot to say Fiona and Natalie were very real as old men and Hilary did great stuff with her eyes and the kids in the time capsule were cool.

"Yeah, they're doin' a good job," Philip said. Then he muttered to Wesley, "I hope that makes up for it being a lame idea."

"So, we only have one more rehearsal," Natalie said.

"No, this was it," Mrs. Reinhold said. "Tomorrow we are having a special lunch in honor of your hard work. Don't bring your brown bag. I am providing a sumptuous repast."

"I never had repast," Shad said. "Is that Italian?"

The college kids laughed. Everybody else looked confused.

"Look it up, Mr. Shifferdecker," Mrs. Reinhold said.

Lily was a little nervous about not rehearsing on Friday, so she took Kresha home with her Thursday afternoon to do the scene a few more times. Mom had made her promise to come straight home from school, skipping Girlz Club, but she hadn't said not to bring anybody over.

Kresha and Lily were practicing in her room when she heard Mom come in downstairs. That was just about the time when Kresha was backing her onto the couch, and Lily went into a coughing fit. She was still doubled over when Mom threw the door open.

"Lilianna," she said, "put your pajamas on immediately and get into that bed."

Lily didn't argue. Mom never called her Lilianna unless it was a there-will-be-no-discussion situation. Mom sent Kresha downstairs for some orange juice and the phone.

"Who are you going to call?" Lily said anxiously.

"The doctor. I'm going to try to get you in first thing in the morning."

"But, Mom—"

"But Lil—you sound like you have bronchitis. If we get you some antibiotics now, you might still be able to perform Saturday."

"Might?"

"That's what I said. Get under those covers. I'm going to see if I can locate the thermometer—which ought to be a feat in itself—"

She went off muttering, and Lily sank against the pillows with tears in her eyes.

It was a terrible night. Lily was up coughing during most of it, and when she *was* asleep, she had terrible dreams about Chelsea and Ashley piling heavy stuff on her chest—backpacks full of the complete works of Shakespeare. Each time, she woke up sweaty and coughed until her chest ached.

At 8:00 a.m., Mom had her lying down in the backseat of the van, headed for Dr. Fernandez's office.

"If I get antibiotics, can I still go to school for lunch?" Lily said.

Mom frowned into the rearview mirror. "Don't get your hopes up, Lil. You're sicker than any of the rest of us were—sicker than I've ever seen you."

Dr. Fernandez took one listen at Lily's chest and ordered an X-ray. Within half an hour he was shaking his head at Mom.

"Bronchitis?" she said.

"Nope. Pneumonia."

"Don't you have antibiotics for that?" Lily said. "Can't I just take them and go to school?"

"You're not going to school for a while, hon," Dr. Fernandez said. "I'm considering admitting you to the hospital."

"The hospital?"

Lily started to cry—which hurt her chest and made her cough. Mom pulled her into a hug and rubbed her back.

"You think you can keep her down at home?" Dr. Fernandez said.

"Not a problem," Mom said.

"If her fever doesn't come down by tonight, though, you call me and we'll get her in. This is nothing to fool around with."

Lily didn't hear the rest of the conversation. It didn't matter how much it hurt, all she could do was cry.

As soon as they got home, Mom was on the phone to Mrs. Reinhold while Lily fell back into bed. She was still crying when Mom came in.

"What did she say?" Lily said. "Does she hate me?"

"They're giving her a message to call me when she gets out of class," Mom said. "And I'm sure she doesn't hate you. In the first place, this isn't your fault."

"Then who can I be mad at?" Lily said. "'Cause this isn't fair!"

"I know," Mom said. "And if you want to give yourself a little ten-minute pity party, I'll even come. We'll serve a little penicillin, a little Biaxin—"

"You know what's weird?" Lily said.

"What?"

"I don't just feel bad for me. I feel bad for Shad. He really tried this time. He even rehearsed over at Ed's when he didn't have to."

"Huh," Mom said.

"What 'huh'?"

"I think the praying-for-your-enemies deal is paying off. That may be the first nice thing I've ever heard you say about Shad."

"Doesn't matter what I say, though," Lily said. "He still doesn't get to do the scene. Who'd have ever thought I'd be the one to cause it? I always thought it would be him." She started to cry again. "I feel like I've let him down. Now those eighth graders really are gonna hate me—and I know none of them are gonna pray for me."

"But look at all the other things you've done for this project. The time capsule was your idea. You provided Suzy and Zooey, which was as good for them as it was for the whole group." Mom scooted Otto off the bed and smoothed out the covers. "You have definitely helped Kresha with her confidence. I love watching her rehearse with you — she's a hoot!"

Mom stopped. She turned slowly to look at Lily, but Lily was way ahead of her.

"Mom!" Lily said. "That's it! Kresha could take my place. She could even fit into the costume!"

"She knows Shad's part, but does she know yours?"

"Yeah!" Lily said. "We both know the whole scene — we did it enough times!"

"It sure sounds like a good idea."

"Mom —" Lily sat up and grabbed both of her mother's hands. "We gotta pray."

Mom agreed. They prayed together for everything — for Mrs. R to be wise and for Lily to get well and for everybody to learn everything they were supposed to from all this. They had just started on Ashley and Chelsea when the phone rang. It was Mrs. Reinhold.

Lily watched her mom talk, hands still in prayer-fold, hardly daring to hope. But after Mom told Mrs. R their idea, she listened — for what seemed like a whole lifetime — and then she winked at Lily and nodded.

When she hung up, Lily squealed so high it made her cough.

"She's going to round everybody up and see how the scene goes at lunchtime," Mom said. "She'll call us back and let us know if it's a go."

Lily wanted to squeal again, but Mom put the kibosh on that and told Lily she had to take a nap.

Lily was sure she'd never sleep until they heard from Mrs. Reinhold, but Mom was barely out of the room before she dozed off. When she woke up, Mom was there again, grinning.

"Mrs. R said the scene went splendidly, and Kresha is set for tomorrow."

"Wow," Lily said. Then she cried herself back to sleep. She wasn't sure if the tears were happy ones or sad.

From then until Saturday morning, Lily mostly took medicine, drank juice, and slept. Her fever broke around suppertime Friday, which meant no hospital, and Lily was happy about that. But at 9:00 o'clock Saturday morning she was wide awake, imagining everything that was happening right now at the festival. As happy as she was for Shad and Kresha and everyone else, she also felt like they were all at a party she hadn't been invited to. It ached in her chest, right next to the pneumonia.

Mom and Dad tried to cheer her up. They got Art and Joe into her room and brought in a big board, which they set up at the end of Lily's bed and unveiled.

"What's that?" Joe said.

Art and Lily exchanged glances. Art's said, *What did I tell you?*

"This is the plan for a new addition to our house," Dad said.

"This is what you're doing with all that extra money?" Joe said. He wasn't even trying to hide what was obviously disappointment.

"You see that the family room will be a lot bigger," Dad said, "and this upper section here will be another bedroom and bathroom."

"I don't get it,' Art said. "Why do we need another bedroom?"

It was Mom and Dad's turn to trade looks, which got Art raising his eyebrow at Lily. She had to shrug. She'd been so busy with the play, she hadn't even bothered to try to find out what was going on.

"We've been thinking about this for some time," Dad said. "And we've decided that we all have so much as a family that we need to share it with someone who doesn't have what we have."

"You're gonna rent out a room?" Art said.

"Yeah—to an athlete from the college!" Joe said.

"Very creative," Mom said. "But no."

"We're considering adopting another child," Dad said.

Joe's brown eyes bulged. "You're gettin' a baby?"

"Bite your tongue off!" Mom said. "No—this would be a child of at least eight or nine, probably a girl." She winked at Lily. "We need to even things up around here."

The three kids stared at their parents, in a moment quieter than any Lily had ever experienced with them before. Art was the first one to come out of shock.

"I guess that's cool," he said. "I'm not going to be here that much longer anyway."

"I am!" Joe said. "And now I gotta put up with *two* sisters?" He looked as if he'd rather Mom and Dad put *him* up for adoption.

Only Lily was smiling. "A sister?" she said. "I finally get to have a little sister?"

"Oh, man," Art said. "Keep the kid away from Lily or she'll turn into a wacko." But he grinned and tugged at Lily's bed-tangled hair. "She'll be a pretty decent wacko, though."

It was a lot to think about, and Lily did, long after Mom and Dad carted the blueprint away with Joe following behind, begging them to consider a Porsche instead. But even the prospect of another girl in the family didn't replace Lily's visions of all she was missing. The Shakespeare group would be done with the scenes about now and everybody would be having lunch and talking about the awards that would be given out in the afternoon.

They probably aren't even thinking about me, Lily thought. *Except maybe Suzy and Zooey and Kresha. I bet the eighth graders are actually glad I got sick.*

Those were the unhappy thoughts she went to sleep with after she picked at her chicken noodle soup. Mom woke her up sometime later, and Lily opened her eyes to see her holding out Lily's bathrobe.

"Your dad's going to carry you down to the family room."

"Why?"

"Because you're about to have company."

"My new sister already?"

Mom chuckled. "The drugs are affecting your brain, Lil."

No matter how many questions Lily asked them, Mom and Dad refused to tell her who was coming as they propped her up on the couch in the family room and wrapped her in afghans. By the time she heard car doors slamming, she was almost crazy with the suspense. When Mom and Dad went to the front door, Lily said, "Joe—look out the window and tell me who it is."

"How much is it worth to you?" he said, but he went to the window anyway. "It's a bunch of weirdos dressed up in costumes. Somebody didn't tell 'em Halloween's over."

"What kind of costumes?" Lily said.

"The guys have on tights," Joe said. "Dude—you wouldn't get me in those!"

"Is it the Shakespeare kids?" Lily said. "Coming here?"

"Some dude's got on a big purple hat," Joe said.

"It's them!" Lily said.

"Then I'm outta here," Joe said.

"Not me, man," Art said as Joe bolted through the dining room. "Mrs. Reinhold's bringing up the rear with a cake." Art grunted. "That woman hasn't changed a bit."

And then Kresha appeared in the family room doorway, hair in curls, face beaming, glorious in the hot pink velvet dress.

" 'Good morrow, Kate!' " she said. " 'For that's your name, I hear!' "

118

Lily started to clap, but when the entire rest of the Shakespeare group filed in, she froze — and she knew her eyes were popping from her head.

They were all there, including Ed and Victoria and the other college coaches and Suzy and Zooey. Mrs. Reinhold did have a cake, which she handed off to Mom. Shad was carrying something that he immediately stuck behind a chair.

"I'm afraid we don't have enough seats for everyone," Dad said.

But everybody looked too excited to sit down. They all talked at once, until Ed whistled through his fingers and Mrs. Reinhold told them to speak one at a time, the way they'd practiced it.

"We were the hit of the festival!" Wesley said.

"Kresha was adorable!" Hilary said.

"And line-perfect," Victoria put in.

"We all got T-shirts for being amazing," Philip said. "Here's yours."

He presented Lily with a purple T-shirt with a funky picture of Shakespeare on the front and a bunch of signatures all over it.

"We all signed it," Zooey said.

But before Lily could even start to read, other people were piling stuff onto her lap — a certificate of participation — a program — a Polaroid picture of the whole group bowing on stage. Lily was starting to fight back tears — until Natalie and Fiona crowded up to the couch.

"You're not gonna believe this," Natalie said. "But the judges thought our time capsule theme was the most creative thing of the whole day."

"Go figure," Fiona said.

"We told 'em it was your idea," Wesley said. "Everybody in the place gave you a standing ovation."

"Nuh-uh!" Lily said.

Gary flicked another Polaroid into her lap, a picture of a theater full of people on their feet, clapping. "Here's proof," he said.

"So we figured we should give you the ribbon," Natalie said. She produced a blue ribbon with a rosette almost as big around as a paper plate. MOST CREATIVE, it said in gold glitter.

"I feel really stupid now for putting down your idea," Fiona said. "I must be, like, this totally boring person."

"No one in this group qualifies as boring," Mrs. Reinhold said. "Everyone received a second- or third-place ribbon for some skill, Lilianna."

"Except for Shad," Natalie said.

Lily felt a pang. Why was it Natalie could be so nice one minute and so evil the next? Lily sighed. She was going to require a lot more prayer. Meanwhile, poor Shad—

"Tell her, Shad, my man," Ed said.

He gave Shad a shove, and Shad stumbled against the end of the couch. He held up a blue ribbon with BEST ACTOR emblazoned on it.

"Is that yours?" Lily said.

"Yeah," Shad said. And then he started to grin. "When ya got it, ya got it."

There was a chorus of groans, and Ed got Shad in a headlock.

"Tell her the rest," he said.

"Oh, yeah." Shad looked at Lily and then looked at the ceiling. "I wouldn't a been so good if it wouldn't a been for Ed—and you." He glanced down long enough to point at Lily.

"But you did the scene with Kresha," Lily said.

"Yeah, but you taught her. You're weird—but you still oughta be, like, a real actress or something."

"But we all decided we aren't gonna call you weird anymore," Natalie said.

Heads nodded all around the family room. Lily could only look from one to the other.

"Since you're definitely not like most people, though," Philip said, his round face beaming, "we decided to call you unique."

"Excellent word," Mrs. Reinhold said.

"There's one more thing," Fiona said. "Where's the trophy?"

"You carried it in," Natalie said to Shad. "Did you lose it? I told you he'd lose it."

"It's here," Victoria said. She reached behind the chair and handed a huge brass statue of Shakespeare over to Shad, who hoisted it up over his head as Fiona stepped up beside him. Everybody else gathered behind them, as if they'd rehearsed it.

"We got the prize for the best overall performance," Natalie said. "And that wouldn't of happened if you hadn't worked so hard and come up with the theme and brought in prop and costume people and made us all realize we should be practicing at home." She took a breath and looked back at Wesley.

"So," Wesley said, "we decided you get to keep the trophy here 'til you get well and come back to school."

"Then Mrs. Reinhold's gonna present it to all of us again," Philip said, "at a big assembly."

"And at the assembly," Hilary said, "we're gonna do all our scenes again."

"For the entire school—"

"And you get to do it this time—"

"And we're gonna have lights—"

It was hard to tell where one person's voice left off and another picked up, but that was okay. Lily just hugged the trophy to her and cried and laughed—and felt accepted. Unique—but one of the group. It was the best prize ever. Even better than thunderous applause.

They all stayed for cake and were almost finished when Lily realized Suzy, Zooey, and Krcsha had left the room.

"Where are the Girlz?" Lily said to Mom.

"They'll be back," Mom said.

They didn't return, however, until everyone else was gone. When they did, Zooey was carrying a book under her arm.

"What's that?" Lily said.

"Present for you, Lily!" Kresha said. She was already clapping her hands, she was so excited.

"Another present?" Lily said.

"This one's just from us," Zooey said, placing the book in Lily's lap.

LIGHTS! ACTION! LILY! it said on the front in gold stick-on letters.

Lily opened it up. A picture of herself in the wonderful velvet dress smiled back at her.

"It's all the pictures I took during rehearsals," Zooey said. "In the back — see — are the ones I just took today. My mom took 'em to the photo store right after the play this morning."

Zooey was right. The whole book was filled with photographs — of Lily and Kresha practicing on the bench, of Lily and Shad in the "studio," of the whole group painting the time capsule. Every important moment was recorded, along with Zooey's funny comments and quotes from the scene. Everybody gathered around to look at it, even Joe. When he saw the shot of Lily pushing Shad with her foot, he actually said, "Cool!"

When Mom said it was time for Lily to get quiet again, Lily took the scrapbook to bed with her, along with the ribbon and the T-shirt. Mom drew the line at the trophy, and set it on the desk so Lily could see it. When the door was closed and Otto had curled up behind her knees, Lily let out a long, happy sigh.

"Thank you, God," she whispered. "You made it so Shad and Natalie and Fiona and the rest of them aren't my enemies anymore."

Mom had been right. It *was* hard to hate the people you prayed for.

Since that was the case, Lily closed her eyes to pray for Ashley and Chelsea. After all, God *did* work miracles.

Lily Rules!

Nancy Rue

Chapter 1

"All right, guys," Ms. Ferringer said shrilly into the microphone. "Let's settle down now. You guys in the back—take your seats—we need to get started."

Lily Robbins looked around her and shook her head of wildly curly red hair. "Like anybody's listening to her," she said to her best friend, Reni Johnson, who was sitting next to her in the auditorium.

Reni pursed her lips, popping out her dimples. "She might as well be talking to a bunch of animals," she said.

"She is."

Lily pointed to the small group of seventh graders who had been arranging themselves into seats three rows down for the last ten minutes. Ashley Adamson was trying to place everybody boy-girl, amid much flipping of turned-up blonde hair and rolling of heavily shadowed blue eyes. Her cohort, Chelsea Gordon, was plucking at the boys' shirtsleeves and laughing up into their faces—practically drooling as far as Lily could tell.

"She's gotta be the worst flirt in the whole seventh grade," said Zooey Hoffman, who was sitting on the other side of Lily.

On the other side of Zooey, Suzy Wheeler shook her head, her shiny, straight black hair splashing against her cheeks. "Bernadette's worse."

Lily had to strain to hear Suzy, who was obviously trying to follow Ms. Ferringer's instructions even though none of the other students were.

"What Suzy say?"

That came from Kresha Ragina, who was sitting on the other side of Reni, squinting from behind her wispy, sand-colored bangs.

This has got to be hard for Kresha, Lily thought.

Kresha was from Croatia, and although her English was improving all the time, she still had trouble sorting out words when there was chaos.

"She said Bernadette is the biggest flirt in the seventh grade," Reni told her.

"What is 'flirt'?"

Lily let Reni explain it to Kresha while she studied Bernadette. She was definitely tossing her head of shoulder-length, curling-ironed hair at Benjamin. But she had some pretty stiff competition from Chelsea and Ashley and about five other girls who were all snatching ball caps from the heads of boys who, they obviously knew, would go to great lengths to get them back.

What is so fun about being around a bunch of absurd little creeps? Lily thought. *Give me my Girlz anytime.*

She looked down the row on either side of her at Suzy, Zooey, Reni, and Kresha—the Girlz Only Club—and gave a contented sigh. Just then the microphone squawked with feedback up on the stage, which sent everybody into a frenzy of moaning and ear covering. Ms. Ferringer took that opportunity to shout, "Quiet down now, guys, or we won't get any class officers elected today."

At that, Ashley half-rose in her seat and made a loud shushing noise. The auditorium got as quiet as it was probably going to get.

"She *so* thinks she runs this school," Zooey whispered to Lily, round eyes rolling.

Lily rolled hers back and then settled into the seat. This was going to be a long assembly, watching the popular kids get elected to office. It was going to give them still another reason to act like they owned Cedar Hills Middle School.

"We're three months into the school year," Ms. Ferringer said into the mike.

"Ya think?" somebody in Ashley's row shouted.

A bunch of kids laughed. Lily didn't.

"And now that you've all had a chance to get to know people who've come here from other elementary schools, you get to elect officers."

"She talks like one of the kids," Reni whispered to Lily. "No wonder she doesn't have any control."

Lily nodded. Even now in the row in front of them, Daniel and Leo were launching folded-up pieces of paper from rubber bands.

"Here's how this is going to work, guys," Ms. Ferringer was shouting, even though she was practically swallowing the microphone at this point. "Quiet down now—I will take nominations for president first."

Hands went up in Ashley's row, and somebody yelled out "Benjamin!" The rest of them clapped like the voting had already happened.

"If you nominate someone," Ms. Ferringer went on, "you have to give a nominating speech—not longer than a minute—about why you think your candidate would make a good officer."

Bernadette waved her hand more wildly than ever. Ms. Ferringer pointed to her, and Bernadette bounced out of her seat and up the aisle toward the stage, hair swinging down her back in perfect curls.

"I want to nominate Benjamin!" Bernadette squealed into the mike. Ashley's row erupted.

Ms. Ferringer paused, dry-erase marker in her hand. "What is Benjamin's last name?" she asked.

Bernadette looked at her as if she'd lost her mind. "Hel-lo-o," she said. "Weeks!"

"Like everybody in the world knows him," Reni muttered to Lily.

While Ms. Ferringer wrote Benjamin's name on the whiteboard, Bernadette dazzled the auditorium with a smile and said, "I nominate Benjamin because — he's so cute!" Then she squealed again and tossed her hair. "No — just kidding — I mean, he *is* cute — but that's not why he should be president. He should be president because — like — who else knows as many people as he does?"

Ashley's row cheered as if Bernadette had just delivered the Gettysburg Address, and Bernadette bounced back to her seat.

"Any other nominations?" Ms. Ferringer said.

To Lily's surprise, Ashley raised her hand.

"Who's she gonna nominate?" Reni whispered to Lily. "I thought her whole crowd would be voting for Benjamin."

"Come on up," Ms. Ferringer said to Ashley. Although the auditorium was still one big squirming mass, she looked pleased, as if things were going rather well. Lily looked at the clock. They still had fifty endless minutes to go.

When Ashley got to the microphone, she took a few seconds to connect with her group, who all whistled and cheered before she even said anything. Then she leaned into the mike, gave a somewhat evil smile, and said, "I nominate Lily Robbins."

Lily immediately knew she was starting to blotch up like she always did when she wanted to crawl into a hole and die. Ashley would do *anything* to humiliate Lily.

"I think Lily Robbins should be president," Ashley was saying, still with that sarcastic smile on her face, "because she's, like, way responsible, and she's totally serious about everything." She paused, as if she were expecting boos. There were a few exaggerated snores and one shout of, "Oh — so she's a geek!" But it apparently wasn't enough for Ashley, because she added, "And she's teacher's pet in, like, every class."

That did it. The auditorium exploded with put-down laughter and cut-down comments. Lily felt like she was being sliced and diced for a trip to the frying pan.

"So if you like that kind of a person," Ashley shrieked over the commotion, "vote for Lily Snobbins — oh, sorry — Robbins."

"I'm gonna throw up," Lily said to Reni.

"Are you really?" Zooey said. "Do you want me to go to the restroom with you?"

"No!" Reni said. "You have to stay here and vote!"

"Like it's gonna matter," Lily said as she watched Ashley wiggle triumphantly back to her seat. "Nobody's gonna vote for me after that speech."

"Will the two candidates please hide your eyes?" Ms. Ferringer said from the stage. "We will vote by raising hands. Teachers — are you ready to count?"

Several of the teachers and administrators stood up, including Officer Horn, the school's policewoman, who was known among the students as Deputy Dog. Right now she was living up to her nickname as she came down the aisle and stood like a rottweiler at the end of Ashley's row.

"She's gonna make sure nobody raises more than one hand," Reni said. "Cover your eyes, Lily."

Lily did, gladly. There was no way she wanted to see how badly she was about to be defeated.

"All those for Benjamin raise your hands, please," Ms. Ferringer said.

Lily could feel arms waving in front of her and behind her. She could also hear Ashley's friends giving a victory whoop.

"All those for Lily —"

There was a lot of rustling around — more than Lily expected — and beside her, she heard Reni gasp.

"Lily!" she whispered. "I think you just won!"

Lily shook her head. "No way!" she whispered back.

There was a long, unbearable pause, and then Ms. Ferringer cried out, "Lily Robbins is our seventh-grade class president!"

She sounded as amazed as Lily felt. Lily pulled her hands away from her eyes and looked around, stunned. The first person she saw was Ashley, popping up out of her seat.

"That's not right!" she shouted. "We demand a—" She turned abruptly to her friends. "What's that thing called?" she said.

"A recount!" Benjamin called out.

Ms. Ferringer hesitated, as if she were considering it. Down in the front, Mrs. Reinhold—the English teacher—was shaking her head firmly. Ms. Ferringer glanced down at her and shook her head at Ashley.

"She's as scared of Mrs. Reinhold as we are!" Suzy said.

At least, that was what Lily *thought* Suzy said. She was still so flabbergasted, she wasn't sure of anything she was hearing.

But Ms. Ferringer erased Benjamin's name from the board and opened the nominations for vice president. Bernadette was, of course, on her feet at once, but Lily missed most of what went on for the next few minutes.

I'm president! was all she could think. *I'm president of the whole seventh-grade class!*

Visions of standing before them all, gavel in hand, filled Lily's head. She'd have to rethink her wardrobe, of course. You couldn't conduct class meetings in jeans. She'd definitely have to tame her hair—and probably get a more conservative binder since hers had Winnie the Pooh on the front. Then there were going to be bills and amendments to introduce and all that stuff that she wasn't quite sure about yet, but if she got some books to read about government and maybe interviewed the mayor—

She was imagining herself putting some important-looking document on the principal's desk when Reni nudged her and said, "Raise your hand!"

"Why?" Lily said, as Reni grabbed her wrist and jerked her arm into the air.

"You're voting for Ian Collins!"

"Who's Ian Collins?"

"I don't know—but he's not Benjamin!"

Lily looked with glazed eyes at the dry-erase board. The names Ian Collins and Benjamin Weeks had been written there, and votes were obviously being taken. It looked as if Benjamin's name was about to be erased again.

"Ian Collins is our winner!" Ms. Ferringer said—although she looked once more at Mrs. Reinhold for the final nod. Ashley's group stood up and chanted, "Recount!"

Lily ignored them and checked out Ian Collins, who was sitting across the aisle, being congratulated by his friends.

Oh, yeah, Lily thought. *I know him.* He was in a couple of her classes, but she'd never noticed him much, probably because he wasn't obnoxious. Most of her attention to boys had been attracted by the stupid things they always seemed to be doing.

Lily looked curiously at Ian. He was taller than a lot of the boys in seventh grade, most of whom still came up to about Lily's shoulder. He was skinny, and he wore his almost-blond hair short but not weirdly shaved anywhere, and he was currently grinning at a couple of his buddies, brown eyes shining from behind a pair of wire-rim glasses.

Yikes, Lily thought, *we elected somebody who wears glasses?*

That made her a little nervous, actually. If he wore glasses and he was still popular enough to get voted in, he must be pretty cool. Cool was never a word other kids used to describe Lily. She knew that. Working with Ian could be humiliating.

But Lily straightened her shoulders. *I'm president now,* she told herself. *It's all about confidence.*

Just then, Ian looked across the aisle and caught her eye. She gave him a quick wave. He grinned, and it wasn't an "oh, brother, I have to work with a dork" smile but one that said, "All right."

It was enough to inspire Lily to shoot her hand up when Ms. Ferringer said, "Nominations for secretary?"

"Suzy Wheeler," Lily said when Ms. Ferringer called on her. She could hear shy Suzy protesting as Lily rose to give her nominating speech, but Lily ignored her. Suzy was the neatest, most organized person on the planet, which was what Lily told her audience. When she was finished, Ashley's whole row stood up like one person and shouted, "Boo!"

Before Lily could even start to turn blotchy, Deputy Dog was on them, hauling the whole crowd of them out of their seats and up the aisle. When the vote was taken, there was barely anybody there to vote for their candidate, Chelsea. Suzy was elected by a landslide.

From there it was a piece of cake getting Ian's friend Lee Ohara elected treasurer and Zooey elected historian. Kresha gave an adorable speech about Zooey's experience with scrapbooking. Lily was convinced most people voted for Zooey because they thought Kresha's accent was cute. By the time the assembly was over, none of Ashley's crowd had been elected to office, and three of the five Girlz had.

It was the two who hadn't — Kresha and Reni — who made Lily play down her victory as they all headed off for their second-period classes. Reni and Kresha seemed happy for them, but it struck Lily that this was one of the few times they wouldn't all be doing something together.

Lily changed the subject to what they were all going to do at their Girlz Only Club meeting at Zooey's after school. She was sure that made Kresha's smile a little wider and Reni's dimples a little deeper.

By the time she got home that day, however, Lily was about to pop to really share the news in style with somebody. Mom and Dad, she knew, were going to be so proud. And besides, with her older brother Art always winning at band contests and her little brother Joe hauling home trophies for every sport in life, it was nice to be a winner herself for a change.

She was a little disappointed when she first got home that Dad wasn't available. The Robbins family was adding on to the house—in preparation for a new kid they were hoping to adopt—and Dad was tied up in his study with a tattooed construction worker, poring over blueprints.

Mom didn't get home until almost 5:30, and by then Lily was ready to explode. She met Mom at the door from the garage, and said, "Guess what!"

"You got through the entire afternoon without getting into a fight with either of your brothers," Mom said. Her mouth twitched the way it did when she was teasing.

"No!" Lily said. "I mean—I did—but that's not my news."

"That's enough news for me," Mom said. "I may go into shock." She put two bags of groceries on the kitchen counter. "Help me get the rest of the stuff out of the car, would you, Lil?"

"Mom—wait—you hafta hear my real news!" Lily grabbed both of her mother's hands. "I was elected class president today!"

Mom gave the expected jolt of surprise, her brown-like-a-deer's eyes widening.

But then she pointed to one of the kitchen chairs and said, "Sit down, Lil. I think we need to talk about this."

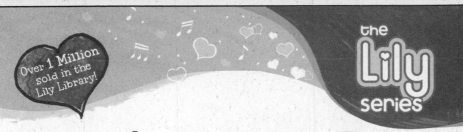

The Creativity Book

zonderkidz

Nancy Rue

Who Said You Weren't Creative?

**In the beginning God created
the heavens and the earth.**

Genesis 1:1

Think back to the last time you heard a teacher say, "I want you to be creative on this assignment."

Did you, like **Lily**, have more ideas than you could ever do and, in your head, they kept raising their hands and repeating, *Pick me! Pick me!*

Or, like **Reni**, did you think to yourself, *Well, I play an instrument, and I can draw okay. I guess I could do one of those.*

Were you more like **Kresha**, thinking, *I can't make anything but cookies — and faces at my little brother. Are those creative?*

Maybe **Suzy**'s reaction was more like yours: *What if I create something and my teacher doesn't like it? What if I fail?*

Or did you fall into **Zooey**'s camp: *I'm not creative! I can't do anything like that! It's a waste of time to try! I'm a loser!*

If asked to be creative, would you respond like any of our Girlz did? If so, this book is for you. Even if you have some other reason for doubting that you have a creative side, keep reading. *Everybody* — that's each and every person ever born — is creative in some way. It comes with the "you" package.

Every person — including you — has the ability to make art in some way. That just means that you take an idea from your mind and make it into something that can be enjoyed, even if it's just by you and you alone. There are tons of ways it can be done:

Baking a cake	Decorating a room	Styling hair
Planning a party	Making babies laugh	Painting faces
Planting a garden	Making up a game	Creating a costume
Writing a letter	Making a birthday card	Wrapping a present
Making a sandwich	Writing new words to a song	Making up a dance
Cheering up a friend	Reading a book out loud	Writing in a diary

Decorating cookies   Keeping a scrapbook   Painting your toenails

Playing with a soccer ball   Displaying a collection   Singing in the shower

Making art isn't the painting, the toothpick structure, or the short story you end up with. It's the *process* of getting from an idea to a finished product—and it's a process that makes living much more fun. Just doing it can make you feel rich inside. The best news is—*anyone* can do it. We know it, of course, because—well—God says so!

HOW IS this a GOD THING?

Probably the very first Bible story you ever learned was the story of creation (you know, the one where God created the heavens and the earth). Can you imagine what a blast that must have been for God? He got to decide what colors roses were going to be and come up with about a bajillion varieties of seashells (for your collecting pleasure!). Not to mention his sense of humor. When was the last time you took a good look at a rhinoceros?

Then, of course, there's you and all the other people he created—each one unique. You don't get more creative than that! Now think about the one thing that sets us humans apart from the rest of God's creation. "So God created man (humans) in his own image." And just to make sure we get it, he goes on to add, "in the image of God he created him" (Genesis 1:27).

What that means is that God made us to be like him—in a human form, of course. And just like him, we were born to create.

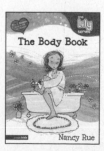

Lily and the Creep (Book Three)

Softcover • ISBN-10: 0-310-23252-X
ISBN-13: 978-0-310-23252-0
Lily learns what it means to be a child of God
and how to develop God's image in herself.

Nancy Rue

The Buddy Book

Softcover • ISBN-10: 0-310-70064-7
ISBN-13: 978-0-310-70064-7
(Companion Nonfiction to *Lily and the Creep*)
The Buddy Book is all about relationships—why they're
important, how lousy your life can be if they're crummy, what
makes a good one, and how God is the Counselor for all of them.

Nancy Rue

Lily's Ultimate Party (Book Four)

Softcover • ISBN-10: 0-310-23253-8
ISBN-13: 978-0-310-23253-7
After Lily's plans for the "ultimate" party fall apart, her grandmother shows
Lily that having a party for the right reasons will help to make it a success.

Nancy Rue

The Best Bash Book

Softcover • ISBN-10: 0-310-70065-5
ISBN-13: 978-0-310-70065-4
(Companion Nonfiction to *Lily's Ultimate Party*)
The Best Bash Book provides fun party ideas and alternatives,
as well as etiquette for hosting and attending parties.

Nancy Rue

Ask Lily (Book Five)

Softcover • ISBN-10: 0-310-23254-6
ISBN-13: 978-0-310-23254-4
Lily becomes the "Answer Girl" and gives
anonymous advice in the school newspaper.

Nancy Rue

The Blurry Rules Book

Softcover • ISBN-10: 0-310-70152-X
ISBN-13: 978-0-310-70152-1
(Companion Nonfiction to *Ask Lily*)
Explaining ethics for an 8-12 year old girl! You will discover that although there
may not always be an easy answer or a concrete rule, there's always a God answer.

Nancy Rue

Available now at your local bookstore!

ZONDERkidz

Lily the Rebel (Book Six)

Softcover • ISBN-10: 0-310-23255-4
ISBN-13: 978-0-310-23255-1

Lily starts to question the rules at home and at school and
decides she may not want to follow the rules.

The It's MY Life Book

Softcover • ISBN-10: 0-310-70153-8
ISBN-13: 978-0-310-70153-8
(Companion Nonfiction to *Lily the Rebel*)

The It's MY Life Book is designed to help you find balance in
your struggle for independence, so you can become not only
your best self, but most of all your God-intended self.

Lights, Action, Lily! (Book Seven)

Softcover • ISBN-10: 0-310-70249-6
ISBN-13: 978-0-310-70249-8

Cast in a Shakespearean play at school by a mere fluke, Lily is immediately
convinced she's destined for a career on Broadway, but finally learns through
a series of entanglements that relationships are more important than a perfect
performance.

The Creativity Book

Softcover • ISBN-10: 0-310-70247-X
ISBN-13: 978-0-310-70247-4
(Companion Nonfiction to *Lights, Action, Lily!*)

Discover your creativity and learn to enjoy the arts in
this fun, activity-filled book written by Nancy Rue.

Lily Rules! (Book Eight)

Softcover • ISBN-10: 0-310-70250-X
ISBN-13: 978-0-310-70250-4

Lily is voted class president at her school, but unlike her
predecessors who have been content to sail along with the title and a
picture in the yearbook, Lily is out to make changes.

The Uniquely Me Book

Softcover • ISBN- 10: 0-310-70248-8
ISBN- 13: 978-0-310-70248-1
(Companion Nonfiction to *Lily Rules!*)

At some point, every girl wonders why she was born and why she's the
way she is. Well, author Nancy Rue has written the perfect book designed
to answer all those nagging uncertainties from a biblical perspective.

Available now at your local bookstore!

Rough & Rugged Lily (Book Nine)

Softcover • ISBN-10: 0-310-70260-7
ISBN-13: 978-0-310-70260-3

Lily's convinced she's destined to become a great outdoorswoman, but when the Robbins family is stranded in a snowstorm on the way to a mountain cabin to celebrate Christmas, she learns the real meaning of survival and how dependent she is on the material things of life.

The Year 'Round Holiday Book

Softcover • ISBN-10: 0-310-70256-9
ISBN-13: 978-0-310-70256-6
(Companion Nonfiction to *Rough and Rugged Lily*)
The Year 'Round Holiday Book will help you celebrate traditional holidays with not only fun and pizzazz, but with deeper meaning as well.

Lily Speaks! (Book Ten)

Softcover • ISBN-10: 0-310-70262-3
ISBN-13: 978-0-310-70262-7

Lily enters the big speech contest at school and learns the up and downsides of competition through her pain and disappointment, as well as the surprise benefits, and how God heals jealousy, envy, and self-doubt.

The Values & Virtues Book

Softcover • ISBN-10: 0-310-70257-7
ISBN-13: 978-0-310-70257-3
(Companion Nonfiction to *Lily Speaks!*)
The Values & Virtues Book offers you tips and skills for improving your study habits, sportsmanship, relationships, and every area of your life.

Available now at your local bookstore!

Horse Crazy Lily (Book Eleven)

Softcover • ISBN-10: 0-310-70263-1
ISBN-13: 978-0-310-70263-4

Lily's in love! With horses?! Back in the "saddle" for another exciting adventure,
Lily's gone western and feels she's destined to be the next famous cowgirl.

The Fun-Finder Book

Softcover • ISBN-10: 0-310-70258-5
ISBN-13: 978-0-310-70258-0
(Companion Nonfiction to *Horse Crazy Lily*)

The Fun-Finder Book is designed to help you find out what you like so that you can
develop your own just-for-you hobby. And if you just can't figure it out, a self-quiz
helps you recognize your likes and dislikes as you discover your God-given talent.

Lily's Church Camp Adventure (Book Twelve)

Softcover • ISBN-10: 0-310-70264-X
ISBN-13: 978-0-310-70264-1

Lily learns a real lesson about the essential habits of the heart
when she and the Girlz attend Camp Galilee.

The Walk-the-Walk Book

Softcover • ISBN-10: 0-310-70259-3
ISBN-13: 978-0-310-70259-7
(Companion Nonfiction to *Lily's Church Camp Adventure*)

Every young girl needs the training that develops positive and lifelong spiritual
habits. Prayer, Bible study, devotion, simplicity, confession, worship, and celebration
are foundational spiritual disciplines to help you "walk-the-walk."

Lily's in London?! (Book Thirteen)

Softcover • ISBN-10: 0-310-70554-1
ISBN-13: 978-0-310-70554-3

Lily's London adventures strengthen her relationship with God as she realizes, more
than ever, there are many possibilities for walking her spiritual path in Christ.

Lily's Passport to Paris (Book Fourteen)

Softcover • ISBN-10: 0-310-70555-X
ISBN-13: 978-0-310-70555-0

Lily visits Paris and meets Christophe, an orphan boy at the mission where her
mom is working. While helping Christophe to understand who God is, Lily finally
discovers her own mission. This last book in the series also includes a letter from
Nancy Rue, which tells what happens to the characters after the series ends, and
introduces the character of Sophie LaCroix from the Faithgirlz! Sophie Series.

Available now at your local bookstore!

Lily Fiction Titles	Companion Nonfiction Title
Here's Lily!, Book One	*The Beauty Book*
Lily Robbins, M.D., Book Two	*The Body Book*
Lily and the Creep, Book Three	*The Buddy Book*
Lily's Ultimate Party, Book Four	*The Best Bash Book*
Ask Lily, Book Five	*The Blurry Rules Book*
Lily the Rebel, Book Six	*The It's MY Life Book*
Lights, Action, Lily!, Book Seven	*The Creativity Book*
Lily Rules!, Book Eight	*The Uniquely Me Book*
Rough & Rugged Lily, Book Nine	*The Year 'Round Holiday Book*
Lily Speaks!, Book Ten	*The Values & Virtues Book*
Horse Crazy Lily, Book Eleven	*The Fun-Finder Book*
Lily's Church Camp Adventure, Book Twelve	*The Walk-the-Walk Book*
Lily's in London?!, Book Thirteen	
Lily's Passport to Paris, Book Fourteen	

NIV Young Women of Faith Bible

General Editor: Susie Shellenberger

Hardcover • ISBN-10: 0-310-91394-2
ISBN-13: 978-0-310-91394-8

Softcover • ISBN-10: 0-310-70278-X
ISBN-13: 978-0-310-70278-8

Now there is a study Bible designed especially for
girls ages 8 to 12. Created to develop a habit of studying God's
Word in young girls, the *NIV Young Women of Faith Bible* is full of
cool, fun to read in-text features that are not only interesting, but
provide insight. It has 52 weekly studies thematically tied to the
NIV Women of Faith Study Bible to encourage a special time of
study for mothers and daughters to share in God's Word.

We want to hear from you. Please send your comments about this book to us in care of zreview@zondervan.com. Thank you.

ZONDERVAN.com/
AUTHORTRACKER
follow your favorite authors